BLINK

TREASURE TRAIL - BOOK 2

MORGAN BRICE

eBook ISBN: 978-1-64795-017-0
Print ISBN: 978-1-64795-018-7
Blink: Copyright © 2021 by Gail Z. Martin.

Cover art by Lou Harper
Darkwind Press is an imprint of DreamSpinner Communications, LLC

BLINK
TREASURE TRAIL - BOOK 2

By Morgan Brice

ONE

ERIK

Erik Mitchell stared in amazement when his friend stopped the car in front of a defunct convenience store. "This was the Regent Theater?"

Jaxon Davies grinned. "Crazy, huh?"

Jaxon ran the Cape May Center for the Arts, an organization that flourished under his charismatic leadership. Jaxon was witty, driven, flamboyant, charming, and every bit as brilliant as his husband. The touch of magic inherent in Jaxon's abundant charisma meant that when he wanted to sway an audience, he could be nearly irresistible. Erik was thankful his friend's moral compass kept him from abusing his gift.

Today, Jaxon wore a navy blue Havana shirt over slim-fitting black trousers, no socks, and custom-made Italian loafers. He might have left Broadway behind, but Jaxon still looked ready to walk a red carpet. He was tall and slender with high cheekbones, piercing eyes, and a magnetic presence that reminded Erik of David Bowie in his Thin White Duke phase. A diamond-studded band that must have cost a fortune sparkled on Jaxon's left hand.

At the moment, Jaxon practically bounced with excitement, like a kid who had eaten too much candy.

"Hi everyone. Are we going in?" A dark-haired woman in her early forties with olive skin and black hair sauntered up, dark eyes sparkling with curiosity. Alessia Mason always seemed calm and controlled, but now she clearly radiated excitement at the possibility of glimpsing the old theater.

Alessia owned the Spirit of the Sea gift shop and had married into one of the old Cape May families, but right now what mattered most was her role as the head of the local coven and the powerful magic she had inherited from her Sicilian mother.

"Right this way," Jaxon said, brandishing the key. "The Arts Council officially owns the building, so we don't even have to sneak in."

He unlocked the door to the convenience store, which was a shell of its past self. All of the fixtures had been sold off, but the faded signage around the top of the walls remained, directing customers toward soft drinks, sundries, and restrooms.

They followed him inside, and Jaxon locked the door behind them. Then they headed toward the back, past the break room and offices to an unmarked door.

"The store was here for over twenty years, and most people never knew that the Regent Theater lay behind it," Jaxon said. He gestured toward the area they had just navigated.

"Imagine coming through the big glass doors, past the ticket booth," Jaxon said, pointing back the way they had come. "You'd enter a high-ceiling lobby with a bar, concession stand, and seating for patrons who came early to see and be seen. Then you'd move farther inside, and there would be double doors leading into the actual theater."

Erik looked behind them, struggling to imagine the way it had once been. A grid of acoustic panels hid the original molded plaster ceiling several feet higher that he had seen in photographs. The plain walls and stained tile floor made it difficult to picture lush red carpet, velvet rope swags, cocktail servers, and a concession stand that not only had popcorn but according to the stories Jaxon shared on the drive over, also served foie gras.

Jaxon opened the door and reached inside to flip on a light. Erik hesitated to get a psychic read on the space ahead.

"Definitely haunted," Alessia said, staring into the distance with a glazed look that told Erik her attention lay elsewhere.

His own touch magic worked differently. To get a strong reaction, Erik usually had to be in physical contact with an object. He had avoided touching anything since they had arrived, but even so, the theater itself gave off unmistakable vibes. Both he and Alessia had extra perception which included seeing ghosts, although neither was a full medium able to summon or speak with the dead.

"Bad things happened here." Erik found himself speaking before he realized it. "Dark magic. Death. Cursed."

Alessia nodded. Beneath her spells and potions lay a similar sensitivity to the energies around her. "Dangerous. What happened before will happen again." She looked to Jaxon. "You can't bring the public in here. Not until we clear away the old magic."

"What kind of old magic?" Jaxon looked from Alessia to Erik.

"A curse. Still potent," Alessia replied, glassy-eyed and focused on her magic. "I pick up anger…betrayal—and vengeance." She seemed to come back to herself. "Just on principle, it's a bad idea to piss off your witch."

"Shit," Erik muttered. "Is that what happened here? Can you break the curse?"

Alessia shrugged. "I need to know more about it first. And I'm curious about why it's still active when the person it was likely cast against is long dead."

Erik understood what she wasn't saying aloud. *If the curse stuck to the place instead of a person, it might have just transferred to the new owner.* Fortunately, Jaxon didn't seem to catch on, and neither of the other two enlightened him. *There's no use panicking him before we know for sure. We'll deal with it when we need to—if we need to.*

Jaxon found an electrical panel and flipped a breaker. Lights illuminated the large auditorium, and Erik groaned at the ruin. Age and animals had destroyed the velvet seats. The faded, moth-eaten curtains had come loose in places, sagging and torn.

Erik glanced at the ceiling and saw where water damage had cracked the plaster, partially destroying the three-dimensional molded medallions.

"I know it's a wreck, but I'll show you the renderings of what it can look like," Jaxon said, and the passion in his voice, honed by a successful career on Broadway, made Erik want to believe.

They had entered at the back of the theater, behind all the tiers of seats, facing the stage. As Jaxon talked, he moved down the steps leading farther into the seating area. "We've already got some grants lined up and a way to take donations. The local PBS channel wants to film the remodeling and do a documentary. We have a grant to collect the stories of people who still remember the theater. The stories will be part of the exhibit and also get made into a book. The book sales plus the ticket fees from the memorabilia exhibit will also help raise money."

Erik understood the allure. While he didn't doubt that the project would require stripping the building down to the studs and starting over, a faithful reproduction would be amazing.

"We may also have some Hollywood help," Jaxon told them. "Not only were movies screened here, but more than you might think were shot in Cape May. I've put the touch on some old friends to see if we can get props, scripts, and posters donated for an auction. Those would be items associated with the town, but not directly linked to the theater itself, except that they probably had a premiere here."

"Sounds like you have it all figured out," Erik said.

Alessia had wandered a few feet away from them with a look of concentration on her face. Erik wondered what she was picking up from the old magic and how they would be able to unravel the mystery of the curse.

The longer they stayed in the old theater, the more uncomfortable Erik became. Even though he wasn't touching anything with his hands, he was in contact with the old building just by standing on the floor. The resonance had to be strong for him to pick up on it that way, and Erik didn't want to know what might happen if he actually handled something.

He had mentioned his initial impression when they entered. Staying longer gave him time to tune into a second level of memories and pictures that had become part of the old theater's energy. Images flashed through his mind from throughout the Regent's long existence. These weren't photos he had seen somewhere. Erik knew he was sensing them from the theater itself.

Some were premieres and shows from the golden era. Those felt optimistic and excited. Others were of rehearsals and stage set-ups, filled with the hard work of people the audience would never know. When the Regent fell silent between events, Erik picked up on brooding tension. A growing psychic darkness had spread like black mold, seeping into the bones of the building.

"I think we should come back another time," Erik said quietly as if the old showplace might hear him.

Alessia walked back toward them with a disquieted expression. For the first time, Jaxon seemed to pick up on their concern.

"That's fine—we can't go much farther anyhow due to safety concerns. Just wanted you to see the place," he said. "I'll get the lights, and we can leave."

Jaxon headed up the steps toward the rear of the theater. Erik and Alessia still stood just inside the big double doors. As soon as Jaxon neared the top, he yelped in alarm, swayed on his feet, and then tumbled backward down the steps.

Nothing about that looked normal, Erik thought, already in motion to chase after Jaxon. Alessia stayed where she was, but Erik could hear a low chant and felt protective energy rise around them. Alessia's magic pushed back against the theater's energy. Erik felt the conflict in his bones.

"We've got to get out of here," he told Jaxon as he pulled the other man to his feet from where he had finally stopped rolling, three landings down.

"I can walk." Jaxon sounded breathless from his fall. He limped, and Erik got under his arm to help him along. All of Erik's intuition screamed for him to run, but there was no way he was going to leave Jaxon behind.

The tension between the warring magics grew stronger as Erik and Jaxon made it back to where Alessia still murmured an incantation.

He didn't realize that he'd started to jog, practically dragging Jaxon, until they burst through the double doors and into the vestibule. Alessia closed the breaker, and they hurried back to the empty convenience store.

Even there, Erik felt the theater's dark energy, although it was much fainter with the distance. *Could the people who worked in the old convenience store feel it too? Or is it just because Jaxon's with us, and he's the new owner?*

Erik felt the energy shift as Alessia pushed the door open. He braced himself for another attack before they reached the sidewalk, but nothing happened. Erik supported Jaxon while the other man locked up. *The theater let us go. This time.*

"I'll get my car." Alessia took off before either man could reply. Jaxon tentatively put weight on his right ankle and winced.

"How bad?" Erik asked.

Jaxon sighed. "In my Broadway days, I'd have taped it up and still done a dance routine. Screw that. It hurts, but I think it's just twisted, not broken. Some ice and ibuprofen will fix it."

"Please don't go back inside the theater until Alessia and I can figure out what's going on with the curse," Erik said.

"You think a ghost did this?"

Erik shook his head. "You were pushed—but I don't think it was a spirit. There's a malicious energy in the Regent, almost as if it's been waiting and wants to strike out."

Jaxon's eyebrows shot up. "The theater's alive?"

"Not exactly," Erik replied. "More of an energy that's left behind from strong emotions. Think of all of the thousands of people who laughed and cried and gasped at the shows over all those years. It leaves a mark—and that's what my gift can read. Sometimes that energy can go bad. I don't know whether it's related to the curse, or it's because of the deaths that happened here, but it's dangerous."

Alessia pulled up to the curb, and Jaxon limped over to get in the back while Erik went around to climb into the passenger side.

"Do you need an emergency room?" She glanced in the rearview mirror.

Jaxon shook his head. "I don't think so. Thanks. With the way Arjun fusses, I'll have to talk him out of Life Flighting me."

No one said anything for a while, lost in thoughts. The drive back wasn't far, but it seemed to take longer than it should have.

"Is the theater project a total loss?" Jaxon finally asked, sounding more discouraged than Erik had ever heard him.

"Not if we can break the curse," Alessia replied. "I'll work on that part, and Erik can figure out the resonance piece. Don't panic until we've given it our best shot."

"In the meantime, I'll be glad to have a look at whatever memorabilia you've collected so far," Erik said, hoping to cheer Jaxon up. "Maybe it'll give me some insight into what's going on."

"I've already got the boxes ready for you—in case you said yes," Jaxon answered, his usual confidence returning.

Erik laughed. "I'll check in with the front desk and pick them up. Why don't you go home, put your leg up, and rest? Let us do some digging."

Jaxon shook his head stubbornly. "Not yet. Come into the Arts Center—I want to show you what we've already started to pull together."

Alessia dropped Erik and Jaxon off and went to park the car. She met up with them in the Arts Center lobby, and Jaxon gestured for them to follow him as he limped his way to the conference room. "In here." Jaxon let Erik step in ahead of him. "Take a look around."

Blown-up photographs covered every wall except for the whiteboard, which was full of notations in Jaxon's handwriting. The older photos showed an opulent theater decorated in red velvet and gold leaf. Newer photos told a story of decay and neglect. Scattered across the big table were vintage movie posters and old event program books —all of them now faded and yellowed with time—and an architect's 3-D model envisioning the future.

"What do you know about the old Regent Theater?" Jaxon asked as Erik made his way slowly around the room, studying the images.

"Only that it was quite the showplace at one time and then fell into disrepair."

"Oh, it was all that—and plenty more," Jaxon said, glowing with enthusiasm. "Benjamin Voorhis made his fortune in the import/export business at the turn of the last century. He was based in New York City, but he had a beloved beach home here in Cape May—one of those huge Victorians that overlook the water—where he and his family spent the summer months. The only problem was, Voorhis also loved Broadway and later, the movie premieres in the city."

Jaxon leaned on his good leg. "He got the idea to build a grand theater that would attract first-run movies, musical performances, and Broadway touring shows to Cape May—and with them, the upper-class audience that hotels like the Commodore Wilson were built to serve."

"So it was a bid to bring the Nantucket and Jekyll Island summer crowd here?" Erik studied the model on the table.

Jaxon nodded enthusiastically. "Yes. Atlantic City had its boardwalk, gambling, and amusement parks, but the moneyed crowd considered all that too tawdry. Voorhis convinced the Cape May movers and shakers that adding New York City-quality entertainment to the town's beaches, hotels, and restaurants would bring in a 'better sort' of tourist. And for a while, he was almost right."

Alessia looked up, drawn in by Jaxon's tale. "Almost?"

"As opulent as the Commodore Wilson Hotel was, and as top-notch as the shows were at the Regent Theater, Cape May didn't attract the Robber Baron class. They did appeal to the growing middle class and upper-middle class. That brought in customers who could pay for some of the finer things and were less rowdy than the Wildwood and Atlantic City tourists. But it wasn't enough to keep the Commodore Wilson solvent, and things started to go downhill for the Regent with the Second World War. It hung on into the late 1980s, but it never really recovered."

Erik looked at one of the photos of the Regent in its golden era.

He'd been to some of the theaters from that time that survived, and he had always admired their breathtaking opulence. Just going to a show in a place like that made a person feel like a multi-millionaire. Seeing photos of the Regent's decline made him sad.

"What happened?" he asked.

Jaxon perched on the edge of the table. "The Regent closed in 1987, and after the building sat empty for a while, the owner finally walled off the theater portion and converted the front lobby into a convenience store, which didn't last all that long." The distaste was clear in his voice. "It's been left to rot since then."

"Anything can be saved with enough work." Dealing with art and antiquities had brought Erik into contact with a lot of historic properties and crumbling landmarks. "Is the structure sound? Mold and asbestos could be a nightmare."

Jaxon nodded. "Believe me, I know. That's why we commissioned an architectural analysis. The news was better than we expected. The theater's bones are good—structurally sound. We knew it would need to be gutted, but the complications don't look too bad. We've raised money for that part. The next phase is reproducing the interior as closely as we can. And that's where the new exhibit and fundraising comes in."

Erik admired Jaxon's business savvy. He used his celebrity status and leveraged his high-profile connections to bring business to Cape May and investment in the town's arts community. Arjun, the quieter half of the pair, seemed content to write sizable checks from time to time and let Jaxon bask in the limelight.

"How can I help?" Erik had known Jaxon had a role in mind for him when he received the invitation. He'd been intrigued with the concept, but he knew Jaxon enjoyed the pitch, and Erik liked the inside information.

The local theater in the Atlanta suburb where Erik used to live hadn't been nearly as fancy as the Regent, but Erik still remembered it fondly for its faded grandeur. That nostalgia was just part of his curiosity about the old showplace.

"We want to recreate the Regent as a performance space and a museum," Jaxon replied. "I already mentioned that I put a call out to my theater networks for memorabilia, costumes, and anything else that survived. Eventually the pieces will be displayed at the theater."

"And you want me to help authenticate the items that come in?"

Jaxon nodded. "And set aside anything...problematic."

In other words, any pieces that were haunted, cursed, or otherwise unlucky.

"Well, we know for sure that the theater is haunted." Erik pulled out a chair and sat, still intrigued with the model and the floorplans spread out on the table. Artist's renderings showed a new Regent restored to a true showplace. With Jaxon's connections, Arjun's money, and good marketing, the theater could easily become a power-house for the arts community of the whole Jersey Shore.

Jaxon rolled his eyes. "Any theater worth its velvet curtains is haunted. We're actors. We do not go gently into that good night."

"Haunted is fine—but the energy in there is dangerous," Alessia pointed out. "That's not something you can ignore. Do you know what might have caused it?"

Jaxon flung himself dramatically into a chair, which rolled back several feet with him in it. "I'm not sure," he admitted. "There are all kinds of stories. Some are pretty typical—spurned actress hangs herself from the catwalk, set electrician taps into a live connection by accident, sandbag falls and hits a crew member."

"But..."

"There are stories about Voorhis being in tight with the Newark Mob and that he had a *strega*—a witch—who had a hand in his success," Jaxon confessed. "They say that Voorhis and the *strega* had a falling out and that Voorhis killed the *strega* and died under a curse."

"The theater owner double-crossed and killed a *strega*?" Alessia echoed. "That explains the curse. And you didn't mention this to us before we went there?" She pinned Jaxon with a glare.

"I thought it was a rumor to fuel publicity," Jaxon admitted, sheepish.

"Lovely," Erik muttered.

Alessia had been making a slow tour around the room, studying the drawings and plans. "Assuming we can figure out how to get rid of the danger, I think refurbishing the theater is a great idea, and it could be good for Cape May. Live shows, small concerts, art films, major releases—they could all do well there."

"I know, right?" Jaxon enthused. "It could also be used for corporate meetings and all kinds of special events. And when those folks come to town for their event—they stay in hotels, eat in restaurants, buy in shops and spend lots of money. Maybe even buy houses. Everyone wins."

After the every-man-for-himself attitude in the specialized law enforcement circles Erik used to run in, Jaxon's community-booster commitment restored some of his faith in humanity. He could see the effect it had on his friends and neighbors, as well as his own business. Cape May was the kind of place where people looked out for one another—if they weren't hiding a dark past and scheming murderous revenge.

"I agree. I really love the concept—if we can un-haunt the Regent," Erik said, with a vague wave of his hand at the drawings, floor plan, and renderings. "Guess I've got a soft spot for those grand old theaters. Maybe I'll even get Ben to rent a tux." His boyfriend, Ben Nolan, was more of a leather-jacket-and-jeans type.

Jaxon fanned himself. "He would be mighty fine," he agreed. "I could invent a black-tie event just to give you a reason to buy him one. *Buy*, not rent," he said, wagging a finger at Erik. "You should know better. Rentals never fit well in the tush."

Erik tamped down a rush of blood south at the thought of Ben in tight dress pants that left nothing to the imagination.

"You're right, of course." In his old life, Erik wore a tux often enough that he owned several. Much as he enjoyed dressing up, he didn't miss the circumstances.

A dark thought dimmed his mood. "You said the original owner had ties to the Newark Mob. They also had their hooks into the owner of the Commodore Wilson. It's gone. But if you bring back the Regent, is that going to draw unwanted attention?"

"You're worried about Ben?"

Erik quirked an eyebrow. "Give the man a prize." They'd already had one run-in with the Mob over old secrets and long-ago scandals. Erik had no intention of risking their lives again.

"For two model citizens, you both attract the wrong kind of attention," Alessia observed.

"Since no one from Newark's dark side has come sniffing around the old theater since the Regent closed, I think we're safe. Voorhis might have been a player in his day, but that was about seventy years ago," Jaxon added.

"Good," Erik replied. When it came to organized crime, memories were long. Still, if no one had been poking around in all these years, that boded well. Erik found himself crossing his fingers beneath the table.

"This is all fascinating," Alessia said, "but you need to put ice on that ankle before the swelling gets worse." She gave a pointed look at Jaxon, who was trying to casually lean against the large table to take his weight off his injured foot.

"Don't think of it as giving in to the pain," Erik added, only half-joking. "Think of it as sparing Alessia and me the wrath of Arjun when he finds out we let you walk around injured."

Reluctantly, Jaxon agreed, which told Erik that his ankle was worse than he'd admitted. Jaxon made a call to his office, letting them know about the change of plans.

"I'll drive you both home," Alessia offered. Erik carried the boxes of memorabilia out and slid them onto the other side of the back seat. When they pulled up to Trinkets, Erik clapped Jaxon on the shoulder to wish him well and thanked Alessia for the lift.

Susan Hendricks, his neighbor and co-worker, held the door as Erik hauled the boxes inside and put them on the table in the break room.

"Thanks for covering for me. Did we get much traffic?" Erik asked.

"Nope. Summer's over—and all the tourists went home. Congratulations. You've officially survived your first summer in Cape May," Susan teased. Erik looked up with a tired smile.

"I had no idea tourist season could be this exhausting," Erik replied.

"That's why people who live in tourist towns go on their vacations in the off-season," Susan assured him. A pink headband held her short brown hair off her face, a perfect complement to her crisp white short-sleeved shirt and rose-colored capris.

She'd been the first person Erik had met when he moved to Cape May, and he had welcomed having his friendly next-door neighbor drop by while he was unboxing the store's unusual inventory and getting set up. Susan had quickly become a friend, with just the right amount of advice and perspective to be a cool substitute aunt if not an actual surrogate mother. Hiring her on at the store just followed naturally.

"I'll have to run the most recent sales figures to be sure, but I'm almost positive we ended the year comfortably in the black," Erik said, feeling a surge of pride. "I guess that proves that sometimes taking a crazy chance can pay off."

Running an antique and curio shop in a New Jersey beach town was a far cry from what he'd been doing a year ago. His background in art preservation and authentication led to working with museums to identify forgeries, root out fraud, and stop relic misappropriation.

From there, he'd found himself on call to Interpol and other law enforcement entities as an expert consultant in art-related money laundering schemes, which often involved an international cast of shady characters including cartels, traffickers, and the Russian Mob. When an undercover operation went sideways and a bullet nearly killed him, Erik decided in his hospital bed that he was ready for a fresh start. His then-partner had already moved on with another lover.

Erik left his old life behind, sold the condo in Atlanta, and bought Trinkets over the phone. He became the proud owner of a shop with a history of handling haunted and reputedly cursed objects, which oddly enough took advantage of the clairvoyant abilities he had tried hard to ignore. Making the change had been challenging, but Erik had no doubt it was the right move.

Especially after he discovered that he might have had a magical nudge toward buying Trinkets. As it turned out, the shop had a secret role as part of an Alliance of mortals and immortals who got dangerous magical objects out of the wrong hands and saved the world from supernatural threats.

Sorren, an ancient vampire, showed up at Trinkets one night and extended an invitation to Erik to continue to work with the Alliance like his predecessors. Sorren confessed that magic had something to do with making sure Erik saw the shop for sale, although the decision to purchase was entirely up to Erik.

The ring tone from Erik's phone interrupted his memories and made him smile. Falling in love with Ben Nolan was the best part of his move to Cape May and worth everything in his past that had brought Erik to this moment. Sorren made a similar offer to Ben, asking him to consider using his private investigator skills on supernatural cases. Like Erik, Ben had agreed.

Susan winked at him as Erik answered the call, and she moved elsewhere in the store to give him privacy.

"Hey," Erik greeted Ben. "What's up?"

"Just wanted to check in. Nice to hear your voice," Ben replied in the warm, fond tone that made Erik's heartbeat speed up. Erik prayed that Ben's voice would still have that effect on him not just after four months but after forty years.

"Missed you too." Erik liked that Ben was willing to put feelings into words. That was something Erik's former partner refused to do, and Erik hadn't realized how much it meant to him until Ben shared those comments so naturally.

"Still on for dinner?" Ben asked.

"Of course. It's been a busy afternoon—lots to tell you. Did you decide where we're going?"

"Now that the tourists are mostly gone, we might be able to get into that new Mediterranean restaurant that had the long lines all summer," Ben replied. "It would be something a little different."

"Sounds good to me."

"I'll swing by to pick you up at six," Ben said. The call ended, and Erik couldn't help the silly smile on his face.

"You've got it bad—which is really good," Susan said, shaking her head. "He's a keeper. But I think you already know that."

"Yeah." Erik sighed. "I do. It's just that all summer we've both been swamped making a go of new-to-us businesses. We've managed date nights and fun, but there hasn't been time to do the heavy lifting. At some point we're going to need to have the difficult conversations about blending our lives. Moving in together. What each of us wants for the future. I want him to be 'it' for me, and I hope he feels the same, but I haven't asked because I didn't want to rush him. I know that has to happen eventually, but I can't say I'm looking forward to those conversations."

Even though a witch had told Erik that he and Ben were soul-mates, Erik wasn't going to take anything for granted.

Susan chuckled. "When it's the right person, those things all fall into place. All in good time."

"You and Keith navigated through all that?" Erik carefully unwrapped an antique porcelain tea set from its shipping container. Susan spoke of her late husband often and with great fondness. From her many stories, Erik almost felt like he knew Keith, although he had passed on years before Erik came to Cape May.

"Oh heavens! Yes, of course. And it isn't just something that happens once," Susan said. "It's pretty much ongoing. At least it is if you keep on learning about yourself and trying to do better. Makes it a lot easier if you can talk about it with your special someone."

Erik looked down at the packing paper to hide the surge of emotion he felt. "I really hope Ben and I can build something like what you and Keith had. My parents weren't very good at talking. They made assumptions and acted like their guesses were real…it didn't go well."

"Then you know what not to do," Susan said as she came back to the counter and picked up a couple of pieces from the tea set to add to the new window display. "Just take it one day at a time—and keep talking."

Susan's common-sense approach was poles apart from what Erik had encountered, first in academia and then surrounded by the elite law enforcement agents that were part of busting big-ticket art thefts and high profile relic smuggling. Those cultures valued macho posturing and competition, which meant never admitting weakness. Looking back, Erik was still surprised he'd made it out alive.

He nearly hadn't.

"Maybe that's a lesson Ben and I both already learned the hard way." Erik placed another hand-painted teacup on the counter. "Pretending something's okay doesn't make it that way."

Ben had fought his own battles inside the tough-as-nails Newark Police Department when he'd been an undercover cop, and it had almost gotten him killed. They both had the scars to show for their battles, on their bodies, and in their memories. But since they'd been together, Erik had glimpsed a peace he had never thought possible. He wanted that for both of them, with all his heart.

"So—tell me all about Jaxon's new grand scheme," Susan said, gesturing to the boxes. "Unless he pinky-swore you to secrecy? Whatever it is, I hope you're already on board. Jaxon pulls everyone into his orbit."

"I'm not fighting fate," Erik replied. "He wants to bring an old 1920s theater back to life."

"The Cape May Regent!" Susan clapped her hands. "Oh, that would be wonderful—and if there's anyone who can do it, it's Jaxon. It was still open but in decline when I was a teenager, and even past its prime, it had all the old-time glamor. I can't wait to hear what he's got in mind."

Erik smiled at Susan's enthusiasm and her immediate and whole-hearted buy-in. "He's got grand plans, and I think it could be amazing. But there are some hurdles to get over first." *I guess a* strega's *curse counts as a "hurdle."*

"I spent some of the best Saturdays of my life in that place. No one else ever made as good popcorn. But mind the ghosts," Susan cautioned

Erik raised an eyebrow. "Ghosts?"

Susan tut-tutted. "Isn't every theater haunted? The Regent had plenty of ghosts. Pretty sure I saw some of them myself."

"Oh?"

She nodded. "Nothing too dramatic—but enough of a thrill to be memorable. I saw a glamorous woman walk into the ladies room, but when I went in right afterward, there was no one inside. Once when I got there early, I was alone in the lobby, and I saw a man in an old-fashioned suit walk through the doors into the theater—and I mean 'through' the doors. He didn't open them first."

"Interesting," Erik said. "Did you ever hear about the ghosts hurting anyone?"

Susan shook her head. "No. They were more of an added attraction. My friends and I always had a bet on whether a ghost would show up—loser had to buy the popcorn."

That just confirmed Erik's belief that the malicious energy that pushed Jaxon wasn't a regular ghost. "There's something supernatural and dangerous there now. Alessia is trying to figure out how to get rid of it so it's safe to open the Regent again."

Susan patted his arm. "If anyone can do it, I know that you and Alessia and Jaxon will figure it out." She glanced at the boxes. "Now, scoot. You don't want to keep your sweetie waiting," she said with a mischievous smile.

Erik grinned as he walked her to the door to lock up. "You're right about that."

"Have a good evening," Susan replied.

"Oh, I definitely will," he assured her. Tonight, he had a dinner date with Ben.

TWO

BEN

"I'm glad you enjoyed your stay, Mr. Todd. There's a reason the house you rented is one of our most popular units." Ben Nolan kept up the friendly conversation as he settled the renter's bill.

"Been coming here for years. Cape May hasn't failed me yet," Todd said. "Nice job with the upgrades on the house, by the way. That's why I keep coming back."

"How did you find Cape May in the first place?" Ben was authentically curious.

"I saw it in the movies," Todd replied. "*Seaside Holiday, Exit Zero, The Lighthouse Murders*—they were all shot here. Plenty of others too. I always thought it looked like such a pretty, peaceful place, and then my partner Jim and I decided to see if it lived up to the hype. That was thirty years ago."

He sighed. "Jim passed on last June. We already had the reservation for our week here, and I decided to keep it anyhow, see how it went. I worried that the memories might be too much, but it was…good. I'll put in my reservation for next year as soon as I know the dates."

"We'll be looking forward to seeing you," Ben replied.

"You know, I didn't find out until years later that Mob money was behind some of those movies," Todd said. "Guy named Cafaro—a real player back in the day. Had something to do with the big hotel that got torn down a few years ago. Guess the Mob really did have their fingers in everything, huh?"

Ben repressed a shudder. Dealing with the fallout of Cafaro's death —both the human and supernatural aspects—had nearly gotten Erik and him killed. He'd been hoping never to hear the man's name again.

"Glad you had a good vacation—love to have you back again. Always like to have a satisfied customer." Ben smiled, ignoring the comment about Cafaro. He handed over the receipt, and Mr. Todd left with a wave and a promise to see him next year.

Ben leaned back in his chair. In the four months since he'd taken over Nolan Resort Real Estate from his Aunt Meg, Ben had a crash course in all the parts of the rental business he hadn't learned working summers here through high school. He was beginning to feel like he'd gotten the hang of it. The summer had been profitable, and his aunt— who mentored him from wherever she and Uncle Stewart were on their permanent vacation—was pleased.

Even more important, Ben had met Erik. That changed everything.

Jenny at the front desk had left for the day. Ben still had to finish out the receipts and return phone calls before he could close. He glanced at the time and checked his phone for messages in case Erik was running late. No new messages meant they were still on for dinner, and right on cue, his stomach rumbled.

He looked around the office, still surprised sometimes to find himself here. Ben felt like he was a long way from Newark, where he'd grown up and joined the police department. That had ended with him taking a bullet from a corrupt cop on an undercover bust gone bad.

The "thin blue line" was drawn with Ben on the outside, and he'd resigned, disgusted and betrayed. A few years as a private investigator earned him a living, but seeing the dark side of humanity just disillusioned him further. Ben had been in a bad place when his aunt offered him the chance to take over the rental business since she and his uncle were retiring and their son Sean had other plans.

Ben hadn't been sure he'd last longer than the summer until he met Erik.

After the fiasco of his previous relationship, Ben had doubted the "right one" was out there. He and Erik had hit it off, then managed to solve a long-ago murder, piss off the Mob, and nearly get themselves killed. Through all that, the spark between them burned hotter than ever. *If that isn't true love, I don't know what is.*

Ben shuffled the papers on his desk, mostly bids from contractors for renovation projects on several units now that the peak season was over. He was looking forward to the slow months, and at the same time, felt a little queasy.

Over the summer, he and Erik had been so busy settling into their new businesses that their relationship was built on dates and dinners out. There hadn't been time for spending long hours together, having deep or difficult conversations—the kind of things that needed to happen to build a lasting relationship.

Fall brought with it more free time, and that scared Ben. *What if I'm not really what Erik wants or needs once he really has a chance to think about it? He handled international art theft, worked with Interpol, traveled the world. I'm a Newark ex-cop with issues. I know he loves me, and I love him. Will it be enough?*

Alessia Mason had said she sensed Erik and Ben were soulmates. Ben had never believed in that kind of thing before now, but after how quickly he and Erik had formed a bond, Ben was reconsidering that belief. *Even if that's true—and God, I want it to be—we're going to have to work at it. Make it good; keep it strong. I'm not going to fuck this up by taking anything for granted.*

He pulled himself out of his thoughts and focused on a more pressing concern. Cafaro's name triggered bad memories. While he and Erik had solved one mystery about a long-ago murder, doing so had unearthed information about other crimes some people preferred remain forgotten. They'd nearly ended up dead, and part of the fallout was discovering that old Mob ties were alive and well in Cape May.

While they had solved a murder from the 1970s, Ben had accidentally found incriminating evidence implicating Vincente Cafaro in another killing. Cafaro had owned the grand, cursed Commodore Wilson Hotel and had connections to a lot of other enterprises.

Cafaro himself was long dead, but as Ben and Erik had learned the hard way, old crimes could reveal a web of secrets and lies that threatened the living, who would go to deadly lengths to keep the past buried.

For his own peace of mind, Ben had created a program to scan the web for any mention of known Mob players he'd had a role in arresting. He wanted to keep tabs on where they were and what they were doing—and whether they were anywhere near Cape May. Ben considered the tracking program to be an early warning system. Having one of the mobsters he had tangled with in the past show up might not mean anything—but just in case, Ben didn't want to be caught by surprise.

He'd checked the program every couple of days when he first moved to Cape May. Ben might have left his former home, but the undercover bust that had gone wrong had Mob ties—and Newark wasn't that far away. When no one showed up, Ben had relaxed a little —until the Seventies murder case flushed out a local cop who didn't want old organized crime ties to come to light.

Things got quiet again, and Ben realized a month had probably passed since he had checked the program. Did that mean that he was letting go of his paranoia—or that he'd gotten sloppy?

While the program updated, Ben ran a quick internet search on the old movies his renter had talked about. None of them mentioned that Cafaro had helped to finance them, which didn't surprise him. He found an article by a film buff that connected the movies' producer to Cafaro, mentioning the speculation that bankrolling the movies had hastened Cafaro's money trouble with the Commodore Wilson Hotel.

According to the article, Cafaro was having an affair with an actress. The writer suggested Cafaro might also have been trying to launder money, although movies were a dangerous bet compared to less flashy businesses like waste management or construction.

A *ping* told Ben his results were ready. He opened the browser window and scanned the output. The program ran automated searches on a list of keywords and names, looking for any mentions in the news, social media, public records, and some other resources he could access through his PI license—a quick and dirty snapshot.

An obituary told him he could cross one man off his watch list. Another man on the list had been sent to prison. Most of the results had nothing to do with Cape May, which was exactly what Ben wanted to see. He was nearly at the end of the list, ready to relax, when an unwelcome name caught his attention.

"Son of a bitch," Ben muttered.

Enzo Rossi was a mid-level enforcer for the Bianchi Family in Newark. He'd been present the night Ben got shot but had managed to evade doing serious time. The last Ben knew, Rossi did two years in prison and was out early for good behavior. Now Rossi was in the wind, having ghosted on his parole officer.

"Shit." Ben stared at the screen as if the display might magically change.

The racketeering sting that Ben had been part of damaged the Bianchi Family but didn't put it out of business. Fighting the Mob was like playing Whack-A-Mole. Even the Feds didn't expect to wipe them out completely. The goal was to take down the leaders, seize assets, tie up time and money in legal proceedings, and chip away at profits.

Rossi had been loyal muscle protecting Salvatore "Sonny" Bianchi, the target of Ben's sting. Ben had been undercover as a bartender at a nightclub owned by a Rossi cousin—one who had already worked out a deal to save his skin if he rolled over on the others. Ben's bartender persona had hit it off with Rossi, who had been an unwitting source of information. When it all went down, Ben felt certain Rossi took the betrayal personally.

Ben leaned back, drumming his fingers on the arms of his chair. If he'd left the Newark PD on better terms, he might have been able to call someone to get in on the chatter about what Rossi might be up to and where he'd gone. But the sting had outed a dirty cop, and rather than clean house, the department had circled the wagons, forced Ben out, and paid a settlement.

The Newark cops wanted a piece of Ben's hide about as much as the Bianchis did.

"It doesn't mean he's here," Ben muttered. He'd done his best to leave Newark quietly.

Then again, if Rossi decided to look, "Nolan Resort Real Estate" would show up like a neon sign.

Ben debated his options. He could go to Chief Hendricks of the Cape May police with his concerns. Hendricks was a decent guy, and he'd come to the rescue when Erik had been kidnapped.

And tell him what? I doubt I'm the only guy on Rossi's hit list. If he's smart, he skipped town, and he'll keep running. If it turns out to be nothing, Hendricks won't be quick to believe me the next time there's real trouble.

Ben had hacker friends, but even breaking into Rossi's credit card accounts to find his whereabouts wouldn't really help. Rossi probably had a half dozen fake IDs and cards under other names.

Mentioning it to Erik was out—for now. Until Ben had proof Rossi was in Cape May or looking for him, he didn't want to worry Erik.

Ben knew he couldn't keep looking over his shoulder for the rest of his life. Busting criminals made enemies, whether they were local drug dealers or wise guys. If he started worrying about everyone from his past who might want payback, he'd never sleep again.

If he was going to worry, he'd worry about Erik. Erik had pissed off Russian oligarchs and cartel bosses when he shut down their art smuggling deals. Those guys had more clout and money than the comparatively small fry gangsters Ben had gone after.

Leave it to me to fall in love with a guy who's on the hit list of the Newark Mob's biggest rivals. Two warring families...let's hope we turn out better than Romeo and Juliet.

A *beep* from his phone reminded Ben that it was almost time to get ready to meet Erik for dinner. Right after that, the phone sounded with his cousin's ring tone.

"Hey, Sean! How's Wildwood?"

"You know what it's like here—party all the time."

"Yeah, yeah. All those college kids are going back to school, and then who'll eat your onion rings?" Ben teased.

By rights, running Nolan Resort Real Estate should have been

Sean's job since he was Meg and Stewart's only child. But Sean's dream had been to own a food truck and leave staid Cape May for livelier Wildwood. He'd given Ben his blessing and urged him to accept the job—and the eventual ownership of the company. In return, Ben made it possible for Sean to follow his dream.

Put A Ring On It, Sean's food truck, specialized in gourmet onion rings. It quickly became a favorite of the beach crowd, and Sean was already fantasizing about a second truck.

"Don't underestimate the power of the rings," Sean joked.

"I think I saw that movie—it had hobbits."

"Always a smart ass," Sean replied, falling into their usual banter, but tonight his humor felt forced.

"What's up?" Ben asked. "I didn't forget your birthday again, did I? Aunt Meg's birthday?"

"Nope and nope," Sean replied. "Just thought I'd check in."

Ben frowned. Something wasn't right. Sean was the closest thing Ben had to a brother, and the summers that Ben had spent with his aunt and uncle had seen the two boys roaming Cape May on their bikes, wild and free. It wasn't unusual for them to call each other, but something about this had Ben's intuition tingling.

He decided to play along and see if he could find out what was bothering Sean. A glance at his watch reassured him that he still had time before he was due to meet Erik.

"It's just another beautiful day in the neighborhood," he joked. "Erik and I are going to try out the new Mediterranean restaurant where we couldn't get reservations all summer. In another week, the seasonal stuff will start shutting down. It's been busy here with folks trying to squeeze out the last bit of vacation. I've got fifteen units coming up for a refresh, and that will be its own brand of crazy. Other than that, same old same old."

"We just had our best week on the truck ever," Sean said. He didn't sound as happy about that as he should. "Business built at a steady pace all season. With luck, the locals will still want rings when they're not on the beach."

"Do I hear a 'but' coming?" Ben decided to press it.

Sean waited long enough to reply that Ben knew his concern was warranted. "Nah. Just growing pains. A guy quit on me out of the blue, so I've been pulling extra shifts to cover for him. But we pay well, and unlike a lot of trucks, we're planning to stay in town year-round. I'll find someone to take his place."

"Do you ever sleep? Had any fun lately? Been a while since you got laid?" Ben kept a joking tone as he ran through a mental list of what might be stressing Sean.

"No, no, and maybe," Sean confessed. "We can't all be shacked up with hot international art thieves."

Ben rolled his eyes at the joke. "Erik didn't do the stealing—he stopped the thieves."

"That's what they all say."

"And we aren't living together. At least, not officially."

"Meaning one of you goes home long enough to pick up mail and see if the milk's gone bad?"

"Close enough. No one's changed mailing addresses...yet."

"Is there a story to tell?"

Ben shook his head, then realized Sean couldn't see him. "No. Just an abundance of caution. It's what people get when they grow up—it'll happen to you someday." His tone softened his words. The ribbing had been going on all their lives, almost like a secret language between them.

"Perish the thought."

"We've talked about it, but neither of us has been in our places long, and the summer was crazy—not the time to add a move."

"Dude. You have been totally smitten since the first date. And since you smile more than you ever did before, I'll assume you're *compatible*."

"No comment."

"Like I said," Sean replied, and Ben could visualize his smirk. "So now it's the end of the season, and you're still going strong. What's stopping you?"

Good question, Ben thought. He felt sure Erik had also been thinking about the idea, and Ben debated bringing it up every time he needed to go back to the rental unit he was staying in to do laundry and grab fresh clothes.

"The truth? We've both been burned before, so we're going slow. Want to make sure we do it right," Ben said. He'd always been able to talk honestly with Sean. He just wished that Sean could get past whatever it was keeping him from doing the same.

"You know what they say—if you like it, you should put a ring on it."

Ben chuckled, although the thought didn't induce panic like it had in prior relationships. He knew it was too early for that step, but deep down Ben hoped that Erik would be his forever guy. Being soulmates certainly made that more likely, but not guaranteed. From what little he'd been able to find online that wasn't fiction, soulmates in rare cases could choose not to be together. Ben couldn't imagine how or why—and he didn't want to know. He also hadn't told Sean about the whole made-for-each-other thing since he got plenty of teasing as it was.

"Says the guy who considers a whole weekend to be a long-term commitment," Ben returned.

"Wouldn't want to overwhelm anyone with this much awesomeness." Sean's joking reply was one he'd made many times before. But Ben knew his cousin well enough to suspect that attitude would change for the right person.

A beep reminded Ben he needed to get going to meet Erik. "So… everything's good?" he asked again, unconvinced that Sean was being completely truthful.

"Yeah…I'm okay," Sean replied, which wasn't exactly an answer, but it seemed to be all Sean was willing to admit right now. "I know—you've got a hot dinner date. Go romance your man and then have steamy monogamous sex."

"You're incorrigible." Ben couldn't keep from smiling at Sean's impudence. At least that seemed unchanged by whatever else was going on.

"As always. Catch you later."

Ben stared at his phone after the call ended, wishing for a little psychic talent to figure out what was worrying Sean. Lacking clair-voyance, he figured he would have to wait and see what happened.

He just hoped that whatever the situation was, Sean hadn't gotten in over his head.

———

"I haven't even looked at the menu, and I already think this place is a keeper." Erik took a deep breath, inhaling the amazing scents coming from the restaurant's kitchen, and made a happy noise that went straight to Ben's cock.

"Everything's good here, or so I've been told," Ben replied, adjusting himself beneath the tablecloth. He had ideas about how to get Erik to make that sound in private.

Erik ordered the chicken shawarma, while Ben got the lamb combo. They split the appetizer sampler—grape leaves, tabouli, and falafel—and requested a bottle of Syrah. Then they dug into the warm, house-made pita bread that came with three flavors of hummus.

Ben listened to Erik's recap of his meeting with Jaxon, the new theater project, and the mishap at the Regent.

"Do you think it's haunted—or cursed?" Ben asked. Six months ago, he would have believed in a place being haunted since he could see ghosts, but he'd have laughed at the idea of curses and magic. After the incident with Cafaro's spirit and the legacy of the supremely unlucky Commodore Wilson Hotel, Ben no longer found curses to be a laughing matter.

"Probably both."

A glance told Ben that Erik was completely serious. "Do you think it can be fixed?" he asked.

Erik shrugged. "Not sure yet." He popped another bite of pita and hummus into his mouth.

"Aside from all that, it sounds like a fascinating project. It would be great for Cape May if Jaxon can pull it off." Ben loved movies, although his taste ran more toward superheroes, action flicks, and science fiction. Unfortunately, he couldn't think of any of those kinds of films that had been filmed or set in Cape May.

"I brought two boxes of memorabilia back to the shop to start going through tomorrow," Erik replied. "I'm looking forward to it, even though I know at least a few of them are bound to have some shady resonance. The renderings of what the finished theater would look like are fantastic. Jaxon says I'd need to get you a tux so we could step out for the premiere in style."

"That can be arranged...with the right kind of negotiation," Ben said, dropping his voice to a sexy growl.

He didn't doubt that Erik would look mouthwatering decked out in a tuxedo. Erik stood a few inches shorter than Ben's six-foot height, with blond hair, sapphire eyes, and plenty of muscle despite a deceptively slim build. He could pull off the James Bond vibe and look like he was walking into a high roller suite in a Monte Carlo casino.

Ben, on the other hand, figured someone would mistake him for a server. His dark hair and green eyes, coupled with a muscular build and tats that would show through a dress shirt, made him more Atlantic City than Monaco. He was okay with that, proud of his New Jersey roots. Thankfully Erik, for all of his fancy background, was down-to-earth and never treated Ben with anything less than respect.

Their mutual background with law enforcement—and its disillusionment—gave them common ground, even if on the surface Ben had the street smarts and Erik embodied classy cunning.

"Hmm." Erik pretended to think it over. "Would it help if I said that thinking of you in a tux that fits you just right gives me all kinds of naughty ideas?"

"I might be persuaded." Ben moved his foot to slide the toe of his shoe gently against Erik's leg. He saw the flash of heat in his boyfriend's eyes. If he didn't stop thinking about what he wanted to do with Erik when they got back to the apartment, it would get very uncomfortable to sit through the rest of dinner.

"Hold that thought," Erik said with a smirk as if he'd read Ben's mind. "Why don't you tell me about your day? Because I don't think the men's room here is big enough for two."

"Lots of check-outs, some bookings for fall, and I signed the paperwork on a bunch of renovation work." Ben shrugged. "Sean called. He said things were going well, but I have the feeling he's worried about something."

"Maybe he is, and it's nothing you could do anything about," Erik said. "You guys are close. If he needs you, he'll tell you."

"Yeah, you're probably right." Ben munched a stuffed grape leaf and followed up with a bite of falafel. "Kinda related to the whole theater thing...one of our regular renters dropped off the keys, and it turns out the guy is a big film buff. He mentioned a slew of movies that were filmed here. Figured I ought to look them up, even if they probably don't involve people in capes saving the world."

"We could do a movie night. That's always fun. And we can skip the boring parts." Erik gave him a knowing look. Unless they were watching a gripping blockbuster, movie nights turned into wine-fueled make-out sessions on the couch, followed by enthusiastic sex in various creative locations in the apartment.

"Keep that up, and we'll need to get dinner to-go," Ben teased.

Their server arrived just then with steaming platters piled high with meat, saffron rice, and marinated vegetables. For dessert, Ben ordered Turkish coffee and baklava for both of them.

Erik gave him a wicked smile. "I thought you were in a hurry to go back to the apartment."

"Oh, I am. Strong coffee and all that sugar are for stamina." Ben winked. "And I'll never turn down good baklava."

Ben felt a touch of guilt for not mentioning the Mob ties to the movies and Enzo Rossi. *It's not like there's imminent danger. The movie connection to Cafaro was decades ago, and nothing says Rossi is anywhere near Cape May. No need for both of us to be worried. I'll tell Erik when there's something solid.*

He disliked keeping secrets and knew that wasn't good long term. *But is it a secret if nothing has happened? Right now, it's just my overdeveloped paranoia. If there were any possible danger to Erik, I'd tell him now.*

He brought his attention back to Erik and focused on watching the other man's throat as he swallowed his coffee. The bob of Erik's

Adam's apple and the way the muscles of his neck worked gave Ben lots of ideas, none of which could be pursued in public.

Erik caught him staring and smiled with a knowing look of anticipation. Their server stopped at the table. "I think we're ready for our check, please," Erik told him.

"Your place or mine?" Ben asked as they left the restaurant. The mild temperature was a delicious break from the summer heat, perfect for walking. They strolled along the promenade, where they could see the beach in the moonlight and hear the waves crash on the sand.

"Yours has a bigger shower," Erik replied.

"True. But yours is warded."

Erik frowned. "Worried about something?"

Ben swore silently at his mistake. "I was a cop. I'm always worried." He tried to play it off, but something in Erik's eyes told him his partner wasn't fooled.

"Tell me," Erik said. "We're in this together."

Ben sighed. "I turned up some new Mob ties to Cafaro back in the day and the Bianchi family in Newark. The Bianchis, uh, don't like me very much." He explained everything, feeling foolish. Spoken out loud, it seemed so tenuous.

"Your instincts kept you alive when you were a cop." Erik took Ben's hand. "Don't stop trusting them now. If you think there's something wrong, then you're probably right."

"I wasn't trying to keep secrets," Ben apologized. "It's the Newark Mob, not the Russians. If they show up, it's me, not you, they'd be looking for."

Erik rounded on him. "Is that supposed to make me feel better? You aren't expendable!"

Ben swallowed hard, closing his eyes. "I don't want to fight."

"And I don't want you to get yourself killed." Erik gripped Ben by the shoulders. "I love you. Anyone who comes after one of us comes for both. That's how it works." Erik looked fierce and beautiful. The moonlight accentuated his blond hair and the angles of his features.

"I love you too. And—I'm sorry," Ben replied. "There's nothing solid yet about Rossi—just a hunch. I didn't want to worry you." He figured he might as well tell the whole truth. "I wanted to protect you."

"And how do you think I feel?" Erik demanded. "You think I don't want to protect you too?" He slid a hand down Ben's chest, stopping over the scars from two bullets. Ben's hand rose to mirror the movement, covering a matching scar on Erik's torso.

"I can't protect you if I don't know the danger." Erik's voice was low and deep. "Don't shut me out."

Ben met his gaze. "I didn't mean to. I'm sorry."

Erik kissed him, slow. "I know you didn't. Let's go home."

They went back to Erik's apartment above Trinkets. Both men began shedding clothing as soon as the door locked behind them.

"Want you in me," Ben murmured, with his lips next to Erik's ear. He felt his lover shiver at his hot breath against the sensitive skin. "Please, Erik. Need you."

He knew Erik would understand that what Ben really wanted was to feel grounded and safe. Being reminded about the Bianchi incident and the Cafaro situation stoked Ben's anxiety. Letting Erik possess him, feeling Erik's weight holding him down—Ben needed the reminder that they were both safe.

"You sure?" Erik asked. They switched fairly often—both of them enjoyed changing things up. Anyone who looked at them might draw conclusions based on Erik's slighter build and Ben's muscle and tats, but they'd be wrong.

"Need it, Erik. C'mon—give it to me."

They weren't naked long before they reached the bed. Erik's hot mouth and his hard, leaking erection pressed into the "V" of Ben's groin, and Ben gave himself over to sensation.

Erik's tongue traced down his jaw, along the cords of his neck down to the hollow of his throat. Ben moaned as Erik's hands slid over his chest, stopping to tweak his nipples before moving down to trace the *non timebo mala* tattoo. He honored the bullet scars with kisses, turning something Ben had considered to be ugly into a new erogenous zone. Then Erik brought one hand down to stroke Ben hard while his tongue followed the tribal tat lines of ink that covered his shoulder and upper arm.

"Erik—" Ben raised hands to reciprocate, and Erik shook his head.

"Shh. Let me settle you," he added with a grin. "There'll be plenty of chances for you to return the favor."

Erik seemed to be everywhere—hands, tongue, and body. Ben felt the scratch of wiry hair against his thighs, the reassuring weight of a strong body blanketing his own. Sensation pulled him out of his worries, centered him in his body and the anticipation of connection and release.

"Feel—don't think." Erik's voice was a low rumble in his chest that resonated in Ben's bones.

Ben closed his eyes, giving himself over wholly to sensation. Erik's hands were gentle and firm by turns; his tongue teased and licked. Erik kissed his way over Ben's stomach, following his happy trail, sucking marks into his skin and running the flat of his tongue over them to take away the sting.

Erik swallowed Ben down to the root in one move, and Ben's hips bucked, held in place with one hand's firm grip while Erik flicked open the lube with the other. He never changed his rhythm, sliding up and down in long, slow strokes that drove Ben crazy.

Ben planted his feet flat on the bed and bent his knees, offering himself. Erik hummed with appreciation with his mouth around Ben's cock, and slipped one slick finger against the tight hole farther down. Ben's hands clenched on fistfuls of the sheets as he resisted the urge to thrust into Erik's mouth or fuck himself on the finger that had pushed past the tight ring of muscle.

"More," Ben groaned. "Please."

Erik swiped his tongue over the head of Ben's cock, slipping the tip through the slit. At the same time, he added a second finger, and before long, a third. Ben's breath caught at the hurts-so-good burn while Erik worked him open.

"Just like that. Want you."

Erik turned his fingertips just right and caught Ben's sweet spot, sending a lighting-hot bolt of pleasure through him. "Not gonna last," he warned.

Erik changed his rhythm every few strokes. Sometimes he matched what he did with his mouth and fingers, and then he changed to pulling out in one place while pushing in elsewhere.

"Erik!" Ben shouted as his climax overtook him like a ripple of fire. Erik swallowed his release as Ben's hips pulsed, working him through the aftershocks.

When Ben finally slumped against the mattress, Erik pulled off with a satisfied smile and licked his lips. Then he squirted more lube into his hand and sat back on his haunches, so Ben had a good view as he slicked his cock, which stood hard and leaking against his belly.

Ben bit his lip as Erik sank into him, sliding in all the way on the first stroke. Erik started slow, taking his time.

"Think I can make you come again?" Erik asked in a voice filled with whisky and sin.

"Might take a while. I'm not sixteen anymore," Ben managed.

"I like a challenge."

Erik wrapped one hand around Ben's cock, stroking him back to firmness. Overwhelming sensation teetered between pleasure and pain, then settled into a slow-rising heat deep in his core. Erik seemed to sense Ben's reaction, or maybe he read the signs in the way Ben panted for breath and how his body trembled as Erik hit that spot over and over.

"Let go," Erik urged, raspy from deep-throating Ben's thick cock. "Want to watch you come."

The second climax raced through Ben without warning, and Erik picked up his pace, thrusting hard and fast into him as he let Ben fuck himself to a finish in his grip. Seconds after Ben's come spurted over Erik's fist, Erik's hips jerked, and his whole body tensed as he came deep inside.

Erik paused for a few moments, breathing hard, then guided them both onto their sides, face to face. He pushed Ben's hair out of his eyes and smiled. "Feel better?"

Ben felt sated and boneless. "Oh yeah."

Erik closed the distance between them to kiss Ben. "Best stress-reliever ever."

"It is when you're with the right person," Ben replied, sure he probably looked smitten right now, trusting Erik not to use it against him. That was a big leap since Ben's last partner had been allergic to emotions and putting feelings into words.

Maybe it was because Erik wasn't a regular cop, or perhaps it was just something wonderfully special about him, but saying things out loud came easy when they were together.

"And you're the right person for me." Erik didn't dodge eye contact or look embarrassed. They had both done enough running away. It was time to stand their ground when they found what they wanted, Ben thought.

Erik shifted and sat up, leaving Ben feeling momentarily sad at the loss of connection. Erik padded to the bathroom, took a moment to clean off, and returned with a warm wet cloth. Ben reached for it, but Erik shook his head.

"Let me."

His gentle touch made Ben's throat tighten with emotion. Erik wiped away the evidence of their union, cleaning the sticky mess off Ben's belly and then more intimately, between his legs. The affection on his face and his willingness to make the effort just further confirmed to Ben that Erik really cared. He'd had other lovers who hadn't bothered or who would have made jokes to put up emotional walls between them once the sex was over. Hell, Ben had probably done that himself in the past.

This relationship was different. And Ben desperately hoped that it would last.

Erik tossed the washcloth toward the door and then rolled over, pulling the sheet up over them and slipping his arm around Ben. He nuzzled behind Ben's ear and gave him a kiss on his neck that made Ben shiver.

"Sleep. We're safe here. We'll figure everything else out tomorrow —together."

THREE

ERIK

The alarm pulled Erik from a deep sleep, leaving him disoriented for a few seconds. Ben had rolled onto his side, not as closely pressed together as they had been when they fell asleep.

Probably too warm. He's a furnace, Erik thought. Even so, Ben's hand was on Erik's chest, maintaining contact.

Erik lifted Ben's hand to his lips and kissed it, then moved to face him and slipped a hand down to curl around his partner's morning wood.

"Good morning," Ben murmured, blinking away sleep.

"I can make it a *very* good morning," Erik teased.

"Keep it up, and I might actually come to like mornings."

"Oh, you might 'come' alright," Erik replied. He moved closer and took them both in hand. The velvet steel of their two hard cocks rubbing against each other made Erik moan, especially paired with the feel of his calloused palm on oh-so-sensitive skin. Ben wrapped his hand around them as well, and the next few moments were filled with soft groans and heavy breathing.

Ben closed his eyes as he neared climax, leaning his head back and exposing the long line of his throat. Erik loved watching Ben come, appreciating how it stripped away his jaded cop facade and let him glimpse the vulnerable soul inside.

This orgasm was a gentle release compared to the night before, warm and affirming. Ben smiled and opened his eyes, leaning forward to kiss Erik. "Better than coffee," he said with a wicked glint in his eyes.

"Is that so?"

"Oh yeah. Way better." Ben kissed him again.

"Guess I'm going to need to change the sheets." Erik sighed with mock resignation. "For a good cause."

"What's a little laundry compared to great sex?" Ben wiped his hand on the sheets and rolled out of bed. He threw his discarded clothing from the night before into the laundry basket, fished out a fresh shirt and boxer-briefs from the drawers he shared in Erik's dresser and headed for the bathroom.

Watching Ben made Erik think how good it would be to do this every day. *I should ask him to move in with me. We're practically living together anyhow.*

He heard Ben turn on the shower—a retrofit in the old apartment that added the fixture and a curtain surround to the large claw-foot tub. As much as Erik loved his apartment, Ben's place was modern and spacious, with a large walk-in tiled shower big enough for both of them.

I can't blame him if he wanted me to move there. We'd probably kill ourselves if we tried to have sex in my shower. Or flood the shop.

"You know, I saw a video where the two guys had steamy sex in one of those old-fashioned tubs," Ben said when he walked out. One look at him, shirtless and still toweling off his hair, made Erik's heart skip a beat.

"I saw that video too. I'm pretty sure those guys were ten years younger than we are. I don't think I was ever quite that bendy," Erik replied. He was thirty-five, hardly ancient. Ben was two years younger, not enough of a gap to make any real difference. Still, Erik doubted he could twist into the same positions as the actors to get both of them into the tub, let alone having enough traction and flexibility to manage sex.

"Gotta have goals, man," Ben teased.

Erik cleaned up quickly, then joined Ben in the kitchen. The coffeemaker was on a timer, and Ben had poured cups for both of them. Erik scrambled eggs while Ben made toast and checked on the bacon in the oven. They moved around each other seamlessly, and Erik thought once more how right it seemed.

It's only been a few months. I don't want to rush him. There's no hurry. Want to make sure I don't screw this up.

"Wish me luck," Erik said, pulling himself out of his thoughts. "Jaxon's sending over one of the people from the center to help go through the boxes of memorabilia. Should be interesting."

Ben snorted. "Do you remember the last time you went through a box of old stuff? Got us tangled up with the Commodore Wilson scandal." Hidden pictures in an old clock that Ben found and a long-ago letter in the bottom of a box of "junk" had launched them into a dangerous off-the-books investigation that solved a murder and unearthed old secrets.

"Hoping we'll be luckier this time." Erik turned out the eggs onto two plates. Ben retrieved the bacon from the oven and got the toast when it popped up. They took their breakfast to the table, and Erik thought again how comfortable and natural it felt.

"So...missing your big orgy shower?" he teased. They had joked that there was room for more than just two in Ben's shower—enough for a whole party.

"It's nice, but I have a hard time seeing the place as anything except a rental unit," Ben confessed. "Your apartment has character."

"Is that a nice way of saying it's old?"

Ben grinned. "Maybe. But in a good way. And with all the freaky-weird stuff that shows up at the shop, you've got protections built in."

Erik sobered. "Magical protections. Good against witches, hexes, curses, ghosts. Plain-old-human gangsters? Not so sure about that."

Not too long ago, Erik would have said he didn't believe in most of that. Ghosts? Sure—that wasn't too weird. And he'd had his own experiences with touch magic, knowing far more about an object from handling it than could be explained in any normal way. But the rest? Until he'd seen it for himself, Erik hadn't realized that there was a lot more going on in the world than he had imagined.

"Let's just hope it doesn't come to that," Ben said. His phone alarm sounded, reminding him of the time. "Gotta go—how about spaghetti tonight at my place? We can do movie night and then take advantage of the big shower."

"Sounds fantastic," Erik agreed. Ben grabbed his wallet and keys. Erik pulled him into a slow, lingering kiss. "Have a good day."

Ben grinned. "You too. And I'm looking forward to having a great night."

Erik sighed as Ben headed out. He finished his coffee, poured more into a travel cup, and put the breakfast dishes away, then went downstairs to open Trinkets.

When he reached the door of the shop, Erik paused. Ben wasn't the only one worried about having enemies from their past show up—that fear haunted Erik far more than any actual ghost. Ben had been seriously spooked about the Cafaro connection, even though the mobster had been dead for nearly seventy years. They'd learned the hard way that other people who were still alive stood to lose if details came to light—and would kill to protect themselves.

Which made Erik spend a few extra moments checking the doors, locks, and alarm system to assure himself that nothing showed signs of tampering. He flipped the deadbolt and then went to open the shop itself.

Walking into Trinkets always made Erik feel as if a weight had been lifted from his shoulders. He chalked that up to the protective wardings. Or maybe magic didn't have anything to do with the ease he felt, and it was a matter of finally being in the right place with the right people.

His old life had been full of glamor and danger. Working high-profile cases with the top museums in the world had been a career high. Erik could admit now that he had enjoyed being in on the secrets and had loved the thrill that came from surviving the chase.

Until a bullet seared through him. Lying in his hospital bed, Erik had time to think. Long flights, traveling at a moment's notice, and living in hotels had lost appeal even before he got shot. He knew he couldn't sustain that pace forever.

Trinkets felt right. Erik had sensed that from the first time he'd seen the listing online. The converted old Victorian house had been lovingly maintained, and whatever it had witnessed held more good than bad from the resonance he felt from every inch of the building.

The shop had a heavily protected back closet for dangerous objects, where they would await being handed off to Sorren's people, who could destroy or neutralize them safely. From the rest of the many antiques and curiosities on the shelves, Erik's touch magic picked up a muted resonance, the normal ups and downs of strangers' lives, but most of all, contentment. That felt like a balm after the relentless competition and big egos involved in his last role. Erik vowed to do everything in his power to safeguard this new life—and that included protecting Ben.

He was early, so he didn't flip the sign in the window just yet. Instead, Erik made a fresh pot of coffee in the break room, checked the mail and the messages on the shop's phone, and got ready for the day. Susan tapped on the big plate glass window, and he went to the door to let her in.

"I brought donuts." She held up a box. "Figured if you and the person from the Center for the Arts are going to be hard at work, you need some sugar to go with that caffeine."

"You are a saint," Erik replied and took the box reverently. "Thank you."

"I hope this goes more smoothly than the last project." Susan poured herself some java.

"You and me both." Jaxon's retrospective on the doomed Commodore Wilson Hotel had touched off a chain of events that was far more dangerous than anyone had expected. Erik took a bite of a maple-iced, glazed donut and sighed at the sugary perfection.

"Do you know when Jaxon's person is due?" Susan asked, selecting a raspberry-filled donut from the box.

"Her name's Anna, and she's supposed to get here around nine-thirty," Erik said. "She seems to have really impressed Jaxon—and that's not easy to do."

"Anna Thomas? I know her," Susan said. "Glad to hear she's working with Jaxon. She's smart and a real go-getter." She bit into her donut and was silent for a moment. "Anybody else dropping off stuff for appraisal? Expecting anyone?"

Erik shook his head. "Nothing planned except going through the boxes."

"Then I'll watch the front, and you can take all the time you need back here," she replied. "Maybe you won't find anything quite so...exciting."

"Let's hope."

Erik finished his donut, washed the sugar off his hands, and turned his attention to the two boxes on the table. He had traveled with them in his car and carried them to the shop without a problem, but even so, Erik had felt something disquieting. He suspected that some of the memorabilia was haunted or tainted with dark energy. Nothing world-endingly strong, but potentially dangerous none-theless.

He concentrated, but the jumble of items in the boxes kept him from getting a clear read. Erik had no doubt that once they handled the pieces, he would recognize the ones that shouldn't go on display.

The bells over the shop's door chimed, part warning and part protection. Susan greeted the newcomer like an old friend. Erik looked up to see a red-haired woman in her late thirties standing in the break room doorway.

"Erik? I'm Anna."

Erik stepped forward to shake hands. "Happy to meet you. We've got fresh coffee and a box of donuts. What did you do to draw the short straw and be stuck on box duty?"

Anna laughed. Her red hair was caught back in a ponytail, and in a plain T-shirt and jeans, she was dressed to work. "Would you believe I volunteered? Crazy, huh? I'm not just a theater geek—my degree was in theater history. I've been kicking around the arts community in these parts since I was in high school."

Anna's effervescent energy was infectious, and Erik's mood lightened. "Great to meet you. I'm still new here, but I'm gradually finding my way around."

They chatted while Anna ate a donut and made a cup of coffee, swapping newcomer tips about the town. By the time they settled around the table, Erik had already decided Anna would be good to work with, and he could see why Jaxon had assigned her to the project.

"Let's set everything out, or at least whatever fits on the tabletop, and look them over one at a time," Erik suggested. "Jaxon said there was a list of objects and where they came from. That should help if we have questions." *Or need to track down the former owner of something that's cursed or haunted.*

"Works for me," Anna agreed. "Jaxon's got big plans. I don't know how much he told you."

"Big picture, few details. I'm used to that," Erik replied good-naturedly.

Anna nodded. "That's what I figured. Here's what I know—although it could change depending on how the funding comes in. He wants to do a splashy display with the best memorabilia at the Arts Center to build excitement and bring in donations. Great for news coverage."

"Makes sense. I've worked with a lot of museums," Erik said, carefully omitting the details. "They want buzz and bucks."

"Yep. If we have duplicates, some of those will go into an auction to help pay for renovations. And the items that are historically important but not super exciting will eventually go on display in the theater after it's rebuilt."

Erik knew his role was doing the appraisals, identifying pieces too damaged to be valuable, and setting aside anything dangerous. "Gotta admit—I'm excited to see what's in here," he said. "I guess I'm as starstruck when it comes to the movies as everyone else."

Anna leaned forward conspiratorially. "So's Jaxon. Sure, he was a big hit on Broadway and knows a bunch of A-list folks, but he was like a kid at Christmas when people started to send in memorabilia."

Erik didn't have difficulty believing that, and it was one of the things that made Jaxon so endearing.

"Do you have any good stories about the Regent?" Erik reached in to unload the first box. "Remember—I didn't grow up here, so it's all new to me."

Anna gave him a smile. "The Regent was one of the first great theaters of its kind on the Jersey Shore," she said, helping to pull objects out of the box and set them on the table.

"What do you know about the owner?"

"Benjamin Voorhis had been very successful in business but knew nothing of how theaters worked behind the curtain," Anna replied. "He thought managing the Regent would be glamorous, but running a theater really isn't. Sure, everything glitters when the lights go on, but underneath it is a lot of sweat and hard work."

"Makes sense," Erik said, carefully unwrapping a porcelain ashtray with the Regent's name and logo.

"There's tons of scheduling involved," Anna continued, setting a bundle of old show programs to one side. "Tight budgets. An army of people. Building sets is like a constant construction project. You have to be kinda crazy to love it."

"Museums are a lot like that too, only a little snootier," Erik said. The box he was working on had a bit of everything—matchbooks, small posters, signed scripts, programs, and ticket stubs. He looked at the promotional black and white autographed publicity photos of stars famous in their day but who had faded from memory. So far, nothing had jolted him with its resonance, but he had a way to go before he got to the bottom.

"Voorhis had Mob ties. Everyone knew it," Anna continued matter-of-factly. "From what the gossip columnists wrote, it sounded like he was enjoying his chance to run with the 'bad boys.' Voorhis was used to being the big dog. He didn't realize taking Mob money meant he'd been owned."

"Oh yeah?" Erik's ears perked up.

"The Mob wanted him to smuggle liquor for them during Prohibition," Anna added. "Later, it was drugs. Once he took their 'loans,' he couldn't say no."

"Is that why the Regent had bad luck?" Erik figured if anyone knew the ghost stories, it would be Anna.

She snorted. "Nah. I mean, being in bed with gangsters didn't help. But the Regent had enough 'incidents' that word got around it was cursed. There are always accidents, but not this many or this bad. Theater folks are superstitious. Once that kind of situation gets started, there's no stopping it. And the whole witch thing was definitely a problem."

Anna dished the juicy details with relish. Erik enjoyed the commentary, listening closely even as he matched items to the box inventory and stayed alert for anything that felt "off."

"Witch?" Jaxon had mentioned that Voorhis had a Mob *strega* working with him, but Erik wanted to know what version of the story Anna had heard.

She shrugged. "Who knows if the guy really had mojo or just put on a good show? Voorhis believed he was the real deal. Then the witch died under iffy circumstances, and people said he cursed the theater."

"What about the ghosts?"

Anna took a break from unpacking and rested her elbows on the table. "A jilted boyfriend shot himself in the men's room when he saw his old girlfriend out with a new flame. They say a starlet who let the movie business screw with her head hanged herself off the catwalk. Supposedly one of the maintenance guys burned to death in the boiler room. A set designer fell off a tall ladder and cracked his head open. According to the stories, none of those poor folks ever left."

"Is Voorhis one of them?"

"Doubtful," Anna replied, getting up to pour herself another cup of coffee. She leaned back against the counter. "He vanished on a business trip to the Poconos with the actress he was sleeping with, Collette Dunbar. People said Vincente Cafaro shot Voorhis himself, but no one could ever prove it."

Erik felt like someone had slipped an ice cube down his back. "What did you say?"

Anna looked up from unwrapping more playbills. "About Cafaro?" At Erik's nod, she repeated herself. "What's the matter? See a ghost?"

Was Voorhis the dead man in the photo we found stuffed in that old clock? Erik wondered, feeling his heart beat faster. Ben had found a clock hidden in one of his rental houses and brought it to Erik for appraisal. An old photograph of Cafaro standing over a dead man, the gun still in Cafaro's hand, was inside.

"I'm fine," he assured her. "What happened to Collette?"

"She went into 'seclusion' for a couple of months after Voorhis died and then got herself booked into every magazine and radio interview that would have her, playing the tragic heroine." Anna rolled her eyes. "One of her movies—shot here in Cape May—premiered at the Regent a month after Voorhis's death. Collette was supposed to attend a big red carpet gala. She was photographed entering the theater in a bright red dress that was the hit of the event—and no one ever saw her again."

Erik frowned. If Cafaro thought Collette knew too much, he might have been tempted to snatch her, but grabbing one of the movie's stars the night of the premiere was ballsy, even for the Mob.

"No one found a body?"

She shook her head. "No. The search and her disappearance were a big deal at the time. There were rumors that she was buried under the floor at the Regent. Or hidden in a wall at Cafaro's house. Of course, a lot of people thought that Voorhis faked his death and then helped Collette fake hers so they could run off together." She found a glass replica of the Cape May lighthouse in the box and held it up to see the details.

If Voorhis killed the strega, *where's the body?* As they talked, Erik kept digging through his box. He turned up a drinking glass with the Regent logo etched onto one side, along with a couple of cardboard hand fans promoting the *Last Exit* movie.

As Erik unpacked the odd assortment of keepsakes and souvenirs, he set anything with an uneasy resonance to one side. "Interesting.

Here's an invitation to a 'VIP Premiere Event' with dinner at the Commodore Wilson Hotel followed by limousine service to the Regent. There are photos of a fancy party in the ballroom at the Commodore with movie posters all around."

He turned one of the photos over. "Meet-the-Stars Weekend 1949." The engraved invitation he found underneath the photo made Erik let out a low whistle. "Wow. Cafaro and Voorhis put a package together with a weekend stay at the Commodore, tickets to the hot new movie at the Regent, and a gala party with some of the actors and the producer. The guests paid a pretty penny for the privilege, but the event was invitation-only."

"Smart marketing," Anna replied. "They invited a who's-who of New York society, took photos of them chumming around with the movie people, and fed those to the gossip columnists. Once the pictures hit the papers, everyone who wasn't there had total FOMO. And it made the hotel, the theater, and Cape May look like an exclusive destination."

Erik unwrapped another lighthouse figurine. This one was white porcelain, about six inches tall. Around the base, it read, *See Me At Sunset—Regent Theater, Cape May, NJ.*

"That's one of the movies about the lighthouse," Anna said. "Voorhis did at least five or six that used the Cape May Lighthouse one way or another."

"How do you shoot six movies about the same lighthouse?" he asked, looking up from the figurine in his hands.

Anna burst out laughing. "The movies aren't about the lighthouse —not really. There was a romance about the lonely keeper and a woman who he rescued from a boat wreck. Then the one about World War II and a German spy submarine, and another one with a ghost and a buried treasure. I don't remember the others."

Erik chuckled. "Okay. Now I'm curious. Ben mentioned the movies as well. Can I find these cinematic treasures anywhere?"

"Some of the more successful ones are on Vintage—that new streaming service for classic movies," Anna replied. "Jaxon is trying to wrangle permission to do a film festival with as many of the movies as he can track down. He might even do some outdoors at the lighthouse parking lot like an old-fashioned drive-in."

Erik admired Jaxon's creativity as well as his civic-mindedness. "That could be really fun—and if there was a pitch to make a donation to the lighthouse and park, all the better."

"I don't know whether it would be cheesy to include the film with the stuntman who died there," Anna mused. "Since they say he haunts the place."

Interesting. Erik decided he needed to have a chat with Monty Clark, the park ranger in charge of the lighthouse and its park. Since Monty was a strong medium, Erik figured he'd know about any ghosts who might be hanging around.

"Did they do any movies about that old military bunker?"

Anna shook her head. "The Army had all of the guns removed not long after the war, but they did some weird radio stuff there on and off for a while. It wasn't available to use as a set. Too bad—I've heard it's pretty cool inside."

"I wouldn't mind a look at that myself," Erik said.

"After the Army left, there wasn't anyone at the bunker full-time," Anna went on. "There were rumors that not long afterward, it got used as a smuggling drop."

Erik had seen the old bunker from a distance when he had visited the lighthouse. It stood out on the beach, exposed on all four sides. "Not exactly a private place."

Anna raised an eyebrow. "The park closes at dusk. The ranger isn't primarily there for security. In the wee hours, it's deserted. Plus, since it's out on the beach, you'd see anyone coming, even from the ocean."

She has a point, Erik thought, although it was reckless to use a government installation, even if it was decommissioned. Of course, that might also scare off casual trespassers. "Was Cafaro the one running the drugs?"

"There were rumors," Anna replied. "Of course, everyone knew Cafaro had Mob ties, so people might have just blamed him for everything."

Maybe. Then again, maybe not.

The boxes were finally empty. Erik and Anna looked at the items that crowded the big table. Pieces that didn't spark his gift, Erik unwrapped. Those that drew a reaction from his touch magic, Erik left in their protective paper or bubble wrap for now.

Anna gave him an appraising gaze. "Those are the spooky ones?" Apparently Jaxon had blabbed about Erik's abilities.

"Maybe."

She rolled her eyes. "Yes, Jaxon told me. And I think it's pretty awesome."

Erik let out a breath he didn't realize he'd been holding. Keeping his abilities a secret had been paramount in his old job. He didn't want to get kidnapped by the bad guys—or experimented on by the "good" guys. Erik had no illusions about how valuable his gift could be to the wrong people, but watching what he said and having to invent reasons for why he knew what his touch magic told him took a toll.

"I'm looking for anything that's haunted, cursed, or magic," he said. "Nothing in these boxes packed the kind of whammy I've run into in other situations." Finding a suicide confession from a scandal-ridden motivational guru and being visited by the ghost of Vincente Cafaro weren't things Erik was likely to forget any time soon.

"Do you need to take a look at the things I unpacked?" Anna asked.

Erik thanked his lucky stars she was so matter-of-fact about his magic. "Yes, once I work through mine. Out of curiosity—did anything strike you as 'off'?"

Anna thought about the question and then nodded. "I don't know if this is what you mean, but these pieces made me feel a little edgy and uneasy." She pointed out three souvenirs, and as soon as Erik's hand hovered above them to move them to the side, he picked up their energy.

"Wait." Anna got up and grabbed a spoon from the drawer, then used it to push the questionable items to one side.

"Most of the items they've collected are pretty amazing." Erik knew it was just a fraction of what the exhibit was likely to contain. "I love the idea that everything was just packed away in people's attics and basements all this time, and now the pieces are finally coming home again."

"Jaxon couldn't really explain what you can do, except to say that you could read the 'stories' that people's emotions imprinted on objects." Anna looked fascinated. Erik figured that beat having her run off screaming.

"That's a good way to explain it," Erik replied. "Sometimes it's stronger than just a story—because I can feel or even see what happened. It can be...overwhelming."

"What do you pick up?" Anna asked.

Erik wasn't used to discussing his abilities, and trust came hard. He had told Ben because if the two of them were going to be together, then Ben needed to know the truth. Susan found out because she witnessed Erik having an "episode"—seeing a spirit and feeling the resonance that clung to an object.

Maybe it's time to own up to who I really am.

Erik looked at the memorabilia scattered across the table. The pieces fascinated him—providing windows to a long bygone era. They weren't particularly expensive or linked to famous people, but Erik felt a thrill at seeing a glimpse of what life was like for a "regular" person. *That's what this is,* he thought. *This is the stuff a person who came to Cape May with stars in their eyes would think was important.*

Erik closed his eyes and held his right hand palm down over a glossy, signed photograph of a handsome movie star from bygone days. That let Erik get a surface read without getting walloped if the piece turned out to have strong resonance. Once he touched with bare skin...he was on board for the ride, willing or not.

"The energy is positive." He felt a deep warmth looking at the photo, suggesting that it had meant a lot to the former owner. "I don't recognize the actor, but I'm guessing that either the photo's owner had been a big fan or a role the star played meant a lot to them."

"What about that?" Anna asked, pointing.

The yellowed script for *Light My Way Home,* another movie presumably about the lighthouse, gave Erik a disquieting feeling. "I think there's a story here that isn't the plot of the movie," he replied.

He splayed his hand across the cover of the script, and a tumult of emotions washed over him. *Anger, humiliation, disappointment, and betrayal all came through clearly. He glimpsed two men in clothing from the 1950s arguing. One was younger, with the classic good looks of a leading man. The other, an older man, carried himself with the assurance of wealth and power.*

The actor held a copy of the script, waving it around as he tried to make his point. Erik couldn't hear them, but it was clear from their expressions and body language that neither would back down. Finally, the actor stormed out, still carrying the script.

Erik blinked as the vision faded.

"What did you see?" Anna leaned forward eagerly.

Erik leaned back in his chair. "There was an argument—a big one. I'm guessing it was between one of the actors and someone in charge. A producer or director, maybe? It didn't come to blows, but I thought it might. I couldn't hear what they were saying, but I don't think the actor liked the outcome."

Anna reached for the script and nodded when she read the title. "Yeah, there was a fight all right. Plenty of gossip about this movie, even today. The main actor was Jason Corella, who everyone thought might be the next Cary Grant. He had everything going for him, but he let it go to his head, and he started making demands. If Jason was the man you pictured, I'm betting the other guy was Peter Duncan, the producer behind all the movies that were shot here."

"They had a falling out?"

Anna nodded. "Jason argued for script changes that probably would have improved the movie. The writers and director refused to make them. Jason argued with the producer and lost. They had already shot part of the script, and I guess Jason thought that meant they couldn't fire him. He told a friend that he knew secrets that would 'blow the lid' off the whole operation."

"And?" Erik asked, fearing he could guess what happened next.

"Jason died in a car accident later that night. They changed the script to make his part a flashback, wrote him out, and milked the tragedy for all the publicity they could get."

"If Duncan shot the movies in Cape May, then he would have known Voorhis and Cafaro," Erik said as the pieces started to come together in his mind.

Anna nodded. "Thick as thieves with them, pardon the expression. He had to know that the movies were being bankrolled by Mob money, even if he never admitted it. And there were rumors that Duncan was there the night Cafaro shot Voorhis."

Erik felt like he had been punched in the gut. *The old clock with the photo of Cafaro holding a gun, standing over a body—and ledger sheets, showing cooked books. Duncan would have had access to the movie finances. How had he managed to get the picture—a hidden camera, maybe? Then he tucked the photo and the ledgers away as insurance in case Cafaro ever came after him.*

"What happened to Duncan?"

Anna got up and poured a fresh cup of coffee. "Depends on who you ask. He lived in LA, but when he needed to come to Cape May, he had a regular room at a bed and breakfast. After Voorhis was murdered, Duncan was back in town to meet with Cafaro about funding—and the future of the Regent. He had a heart attack in his room and died."

Erik felt certain that if he tracked down which B&B Duncan had been staying in when he died, it would be the same one where Ben found the old clock hidden in a nailed-down window seat.

"Why does that depend on who you ask?"

"There've always been rumors that Duncan was poisoned," Anna replied.

"Did he and Cafaro have a falling out?"

She shrugged. "Lots of speculation, but no one who claimed to be a witness to whatever they discussed."

"What happened to the local movie production without Duncan and Voorhis?" Erik asked.

"It dried up," Anna said. "Not surprising—but a real shame. The movies weren't blockbusters for their time, but they were worth a Saturday afternoon and some popcorn. No worse than a lot of TV shows, that's for sure. But with Voorhis gone, the Regent went through a string of owners. It was the beginning of the end. And without the Regent's role in promoting the movies, the production moved elsewhere. Not long after that, Cafaro was murdered. End of an era."

"That's quite a story," Erik said, knowing he'd need to sift back through the details. He had the feeling there'd been important clues he missed.

"That's what you get when you ask a vintage film buff for details," Anna said with a chuckle. "And you can count on Jaxon to make sure it gets told in all its glamorous, sordid glory. He's a consummate showman, and nothing brings in crowds like dirty laundry."

They had been working on the boxes all morning, and it was time to break for lunch. Erik felt edgy, and he wasn't sure why. The other items that triggered his gift had relatively minor resonance—nothing that struck him as being dangerous. He could work through them later and decide which could be cleansed and which should be destroyed.

We missed something. I can feel it.

He glanced around the break room, and his gaze stopped on a small package on the counter, still in brown wrapping paper. "What's that?" he asked, pointing.

Anna sighed. "Sorry. I took that out of my box and set it aside because it wasn't opened yet, then forgot about it. It must have gotten tossed in at the last minute." She reached for it, and Erik grabbed her arm.

"There's something off about it."

Her eyes widened. "Like a mail bomb?"

He shook his head. "No—but it's got a dark resonance. *Really* dark.

"How about I open it, and you see if you can get a reading on what's causing the trouble?" she said, with an expression daring him to turn her down.

"Just…be careful."

Anna found scissors in a drawer and cut the tape, taking care not to mar the label on the front. She frowned, confused when she saw what was inside.

"There's got to be a mistake. This isn't Regent memorabilia."

Erik walked over to where she stood and peered down at the box. A charred, twisted piece of metal sat on plain packing paper. Anna poked at it with a spoon, lifting up one end.

"It looks like there's paint on one side."

Erik tapped her on the shoulder, signaling for Anna to move away. Now that the box was open, its energy throbbed like a wound, deep and festering. Even holding his hand inches above the metal, the images it sent overwhelmed him.

Deafening sound, a blinding flash of light—then excruciating pain and an inferno. The blast tore into the driver's body, ripping away limbs, flesh, and bone, then flames engulfed what was left.

"Erik?" Anna sounded like she had been calling to him for a while.

Erik came back to himself with a gasp and realized that Susan stood in the doorway, watching him with concern. He gripped the counter to steady himself, grateful when Anna pushed a chair behind him, and he sat as his knees went wobbly.

"What did you see?" Susan pushed a glass of water into Erik's shaking hand.

"What's in the box?" Anna's question came a second later.

"When did the package come?" Erik asked, sounding breathy with how hard his heart pounded. "Who was it addressed to?"

Anna reached past him to fold back the wrapping and look at the mailing label. "I can't read the postmark, but the package wasn't in the big box when I packed it yesterday." She frowned. "That's odd."

"What?" Erik asked.

"All of the memorabilia should be addressed to 'The Regent Project' so we can easily tell those from regular Arts Center mail. But this one is addressed directly to Jaxon."

"Erik, what's going on? You look like you've had a fright." Susan sounded concerned.

"That's a piece of Vincente Cafaro's car—after the bombing that killed him. It's not memorabilia—it's a warning and a threat." Erik looked from Susan to Anna. "Someone doesn't want Jaxon looking into the Regent's history."

FOUR

ERIK

E rik debated whether to put the twisted piece of metal in the shop's safe or in the warded closet. He had no illusions about how valuable the piece would be to anyone with Mob ties to Cafaro or Voorhis, although what they'd do with it, Erik wasn't sure. He made a mental note to let Sorren know, just in case it mattered.

Still, the twisted steel was evidence, a tangible tie to a still-unsolved murder. The safe also had wardings, but not as strong as the closet's. In the end, he figured that regular people posed as great a threat as magic and opted for the safe.

"What now?" Susan asked. Anna looked a little freaked out, but she hadn't left.

"When I was working with Jaxon on the exhibit about the Commodore Wilson Hotel, Vincente Cafaro's ghost showed up, and he wanted to know who killed him."

Anna stifled a gasp. Susan just nodded.

"Ben found an old clock that had a photo of Cafaro standing over a dead body, holding a gun. It and some incriminating ledgers were crammed inside an antique clock and hidden inside a window seat—in a rental house that used to be an old B&B. A ghost threw Ben across the room, and he broke through the bench."

Anna's eyes widened. "Duncan. He was at the resort in the Poconos when Voorhis died. He must have thought he could protect himself with the ledger and the photos, but Cafaro found out…"

"I'd say the poisoning theory seems likely," Erik replied. "If Cafaro suspected, he'd eliminate the danger."

"Shit," Susan said. "Here we go again."

"Let's hope not," Erik replied. "But whoever sent the piece of his car has to think there's a connection between the bomb that killed Cafaro and the Regent Theater."

"Is that good or bad?" Susan asked.

Erik shook his head. "I wish I knew."

"What now?" Anna wondered.

"I want to go talk to someone who might have good advice," Erik replied.

"Well, you can wait until you eat lunch," Susan said. "Because I ordered sub sandwiches, and they'll be here any minute."

They kept the conversation light as they ate. When they finished, Anna separated the memorabilia into two boxes so she could take the neutral items back to the Arts Council and leave the resonant ones for Erik to examine more closely.

Anna promised to come back the next day with another box. After she was gone, Susan looked at Erik. "Do you think this is a magic-and-ghosts thing, or are we going to have wise guys gunning for you and Ben again?"

Despite the serious concerns, Erik had to chuckle. "I don't think we're important enough to have 'made men' coming after us. Low-level goons, maybe."

Susan smacked him on the arm with the back of her hand. "Don't joke about that kind of thing."

"Sorry. Gallows humor and all that," Erik said. "I honestly have no idea. Ben and I thought that the Cafaro situation was ancient history, and look what happened."

"Ben will be angry if you get yourself killed," Susan warned.

"Angry? He'd crawl into the afterlife and haul me out by the short and curlies," Erik replied.

"Seems to me there are some loose ends to all this that might be dangerous," Susan said. "You don't know who killed Cafaro—and there could be people who are still alive who might not want that mystery solved. Most of the talk I ever heard figured his death had something to do with all the shady doings at the Commodore Wilson. If the bombing was connected to the movies, that might turn up fresh dirt. You'd better watch your back."

———

Alessia Mason was Cape May's top witch from a family of Sicilian witches. Marrying into a long-time Cape May family gave her money, social position, protection, and a good idea of where the scandals were buried. Her gift shop, Spirit of the Sea, was a hit with locals and tourists, reserving the "witchy stuff" for a need-to-know back room.

"Erik! Good to see you again. I've been expecting you."

Erik grinned. "You're a hard person to surprise."

Alessia welcomed him into her shop. Erik felt a frisson of magic when he crossed the threshold that was slightly different from the wardings at Trinkets.

"What's going on, Erik? I hate to say it, but you're not one for social visits."

Erik felt his cheeks color. "Sorry about that. Getting Trinkets through its first tourist season hasn't left a lot of room for much else."

"Forgiven," she joked. "If you don't make a habit of staying away."

The shop was quiet, with just a few customers poking around. Alessia nodded to her helper behind the counter and led Erik to a "consultation room" in the back of the store.

The space had comfortable chairs and couches, all in relaxing shades of sky blue and seafoam green. Erik figured that Alessia used the back room for personal consults with the people who sought her help. He sat on the edge of a high-backed couch, feeling as awkward as a middle-schooler on a date.

"Did you find anything about Voorhis's *strega*?" he asked.

"His name was Thomas Ruccio, from New Brunswick. I checked into the family—Sicilian witches. He was legit."

"How did he get hooked up with Voorhis?"

"You wouldn't know it by his last name, but Voorhis's mother was Sicilian," Alessia replied. "From what I can find, Ruccio knew him from back in the neighborhood—a distant cousin. They worked together for twenty years, and those were prosperous times for Voorhis."

"That makes it worse," Erik said. "What made Voorhis turn on him? Why did they have a falling out? And how the hell did Voorhis kill a witch?"

"The last one is the easiest," Alessia replied. "Betrayal. Unless you're a paranoid son of a bitch, sooner or later you let down your guard around the people you trust."

Erik understood betrayal. "Ouch."

Alessia raised an eyebrow. "Yeah. As for what led to the final fight...I don't know for sure, but I can guess what's likely. Money. Control. Wanting a say in how the business is managed—or a bigger share of the pie."

"Voorhis was at the heart of the Cape May film industry," Erik said. "Was the *strega* working for him—or someone else?"

"If his ghost isn't around and he didn't conveniently leave a journal, that's hard to say," Alessia replied. "I think a better question is—what was the *strega* supposed to do? Glamour potential investors to bankroll upcoming movies? Manipulate reluctant stars to get them to sign contracts? Razzle-dazzle the community into letting the film crews do whatever they wanted?"

Erik cleared his throat. "I, um, had just assumed the *strega* was there for protection—in general and when dealing with the other Mob families."

Alessia cleared her throat. "That's all pretty typical stuff. And a *strega* would have seen it as part of the contract to provide that—for fair payment. Maybe Voorhis got greedy and wanted to cut the *strega* out of his due."

That made a lot of sense, Erik thought. Sometimes the most

straightforward explanations were the most likely. Greed and arrogance had led to a lot of tragedies.

"And the curse?" Erik asked.

"Voorhis might have gotten the drop on the witch if his betrayal hadn't been expected, but once the *strega* realized what was going on, I can imagine him answering with a betrayal of his own—the curse," Alessia replied.

"Betrayal?"

Alessiaia nodded. "Witch families have honor codes. Powers aren't to be used against those in the family and rarely if ever, against those in the inner circle. For obvious reasons."

Erik thought about it. If a witch family started whammying and cursing each other, it could go on for generations without resolution.

"I've been going through memorabilia for Jaxon for his Regent Theater exhibit," Erik said. "And since Vincente Cafaro was also a major investor in the Regent and the film industry in Cape May, some pieces from the Commodore Wilson showed up among all the movie stuff." He cleared his throat. "I was wondering if you thought the witch's curse might have anything to do with the hotel's weirdness."

"Weird" didn't begin to describe the sordid history of the grand old hotel. Huge and opulent, the Commodore Wilson rivaled the best locations in New York or Boston. But the property seemed to be snake-bitten from the start, sending one owner after another into bankruptcy and ruin. Through the years, the Commodore attracted flamboyant but shady owners, leading to scandals as well as a string of suicides, murders, disappearances, and convictions. Being owned by a mobster was one of its tamer incarnations.

"Hard to say." Alessia leaned back in her chair. "The curse certainly wouldn't have been the start of the Commodore Wilson's problems. There's also no reason to think the *strega* would have cursed Cafaro as well as Voorhis. Did you find something that suggests otherwise?"

Erik shook his head. "No, just wondering. This whole mess with the theater and the murders and the movie production feels like something out of a TV drama. It's such a tangle, and so much time has passed that it's hard to figure out what happened."

"The land that the Commodore Wilson was built on is a twisted genius loci," Alessia said. "To put it another way—it was born bad. That's why the plot is still standing empty after all this time and why the ghost of the building comes and goes. We can't get rid of it, so we try to contain the damage."

"Is the genius loci sentient?" Erik didn't know much about elemental spirits, and what information he had found was fragmented and contradictory.

"The lore varies. Some are, some aren't."

"Do you think it could feed off thoughts and memories?"

"Probably not—although it could draw from bad energy," Alessia replied. "It was stronger when the hotel was full of people and got weaker after the place was abandoned. That's why—in addition to wardings and lots of protective boundary spells—we try to starve it by keeping people away."

"Okay." Erik mentally filed that away to consider later. It didn't sound like the Commodore Wilson was the culprit this time.

Alessia gave him a shrewd look. "Talk to me, Erik. There's more you aren't saying."

Erik sighed. "You're right. I got to thinking about how the 'golden age' for the Regent ended after Voorhis died, and no one who owned it later could turn the place around. What if the curse wasn't just on Voorhis? What if the *strega* cursed the theater itself—which might put Jaxon in danger?"

Alessia considered his comment for a moment. "It's possible. You're right about the later owners having bad luck. They didn't all get murdered like Voorhis, but the ones I've heard about came to a bad end. Car wreck, house fire, suicide, sudden illness. It probably would have been a good idea to look into that sort of thing *before* buying the place."

"Do you think Jaxon could be next?" Erik counted the Arts Center impresario as a friend and didn't want to see him come to harm.

"*If* the curse was transferable—and we're just guessing so far—then it would depend on how technical the spell was," Alessia said. "Jaxon didn't personally buy the theater—the Arts Council did."

"But Jaxon is the public face of the council and probably the one to sign the paperwork," Erik pointed out. "Could the spell tell the difference?"

"That would depend on the skill and intent of the witch who cast the curse. If he just meant to ruin Voorhis, there wouldn't be a need to broaden the effect. But if he wanted to destroy everyone involved, cursing the theater and its owner would make sense."

"Is there a way to protect Jaxon?" Erik voiced the question that had been bothering him since he'd learned of the curse.

"We don't know that he's affected," Alessia pointed out. "But I can look into it—just in case. I'll need to figure out what sort of spell was used, and since Ruccio was Sicilian, I'll start there. It never hurts to have another curse-breaking ritual on hand."

"Thank you," Erik said, feeling like a weight had been lifted. "Maybe it's nothing, but I can't stop thinking about it."

Alessia's eyes narrowed, assessing. "From most people, I'd chalk it up as a touch of paranoia. But given your abilities, I'm inclined to think there might be something to your 'hunch.' Give me a day or two —I'll let you know what I find out."

———

Erik got back to Trinkets in time to share what he'd learned from Alessia and help Susan close.

"Anna brought two more boxes," Susan told him. "They're in the back room for tomorrow. She'll be by before ten and said she'll bring the donuts this time."

"I knew she was good people," Erik joked. "I might let her do the unpacking while I check on the other pieces that tingled my Spidey senses. Divide and conquer."

"How many boxes are you expecting?"

Erik shrugged. "You know Jaxon—he'll put the touch on everyone who knows anyone, and it'll be a world-class display, as always."

"Good thing it's the off-season," Susan observed. "If the next few days are as quiet as today, I shouldn't have any problem handling the front by myself."

"I checked the orders on the Treasure Trail site, and I think some folks who didn't buy over the summer had second thoughts. We've had a nice uptick." Right now, Treasure Trail was an online store with occasional blog posts. But Erik had plans to add seminars and other features to help keep income steady through the fall and winter.

Now if only the ghosts, curses, and Mob murders would give me some time off.

"Oops—better go. My Yoga class starts in half an hour." Susan grabbed her bag from behind the counter. "See you in the morning!"

Erik locked up behind her and set the alarm, then hurried upstairs to get ready for his date with Ben. He took a quick shower, fussed with his hair to get it just right, and debated whether to shave. His reddish-blond stubble didn't come in as thick or dark as Ben's did, but there was enough to notice after a long day, and he thought it gave his cheekbones a bit more definition.

Ben doesn't seem to mind a little "beard burn" in the right places. Consider it "incentive."

Erik decided to walk to Ben's place, enjoying the pleasant evening and mild weather. Before too long, cold winds and sleet off the ocean would make it necessary to drive even short distances or bundle up like an arctic explorer. He wasn't looking forward to winter weather, but with Ben to help him keep warm, Erik figured he wouldn't mind.

Once again he thought about asking Ben to move in with him. *I'm pretty sure he likes the idea. But is it rushing things? Everything has gone well so far. What am I scared of? After all, Ben runs a rental company. If it doesn't work out, it's not like he couldn't find a place to live.*

It had been nearly a year since he'd parted ways with his last boyfriend. Close to the same amount of time since Ben's previous relationship too. Both still had emotional scars that could probably benefit from counseling, but they had managed to navigate around those hot spots with relative ease.

Soulmates, remember? It's crazy—but that feels true. And if we are, what's the point of wasting time when we could be together?

Erik vowed to bring up the topic as soon as he got Jaxon's project sorted out. If the piece of twisted steel meant more danger from the past, he wanted to make sure Ben didn't get dragged into it because of him.

Or maybe I'm just scared. I like how things are between us, and I love him. I guess that I'm afraid to rock the boat. Maybe that's a sign right there that I'm not quite as ready as I think I am.

But what if Ben's waiting for me to make the first move? Will he think I'm not as interested or committed? Dammit! I hate how nothing comes with an instruction manual!

———

"I brought wine," Erik said after Ben greeted him with a kiss that gave him all kinds of ideas for "dessert."

"Great! Come on in the kitchen—I don't want to burn the garlic toast or have the spaghetti boil over."

Erik followed Ben inside and set the wine down on the table. He'd long ago stopped needing to bring an overnight bag since he had a drawer and closet space in Ben's room and duplicate toiletries here. *Same as Ben has at my place. We're practically living together now.*

The rental unit Ben had claimed for his own had a modern, sleek look thanks to a recent renovation. The huge tiled walk-in shower was plenty big enough for two men, something they had tested time and again.

Erik knew that the furniture had come with the unit, but most of the knickknacks were Ben's, and he loved glimpsing his partner's favorites, like the large Spider-Man figure in the corner. Framed superhero and fantasy artwork showed off Ben's geeky side, along with pictures of Ben and his cousin Sean, travel photos, and now a few shots of the two of them together.

"Need any help?" Erik asked, admiring the view from behind as Ben navigated his kitchen like a pro. His navy blue T-shirt showed off the muscles of his back and shoulders, with some of his tats peeking from beneath the sleeve. Worn jeans fit like a second skin, providing a perfect view of Ben's fine ass. Bare feet were a turn-on Erik didn't realize he had, but now they meant Ben and summer.

"Wanna get the garlic toast out of the oven? The salad's ready. I figured we could serve ourselves out here and not be as crowded at the table."

Erik grabbed an oven mitt and retrieved the bread, cutting it into pieces while Ben finished the pasta and sauce. He opened the bottle of wine, and got stemless glasses out of the cupboard, then set the table while Ben plated the food.

"I like the way we move around each other, like we've been doing this forever," Ben said as he handed Erik his plate.

"I like brushing up against you in those jeans," Erik replied with a grin. "Gives me lots of inspiration."

"Hold that thought—because tonight is movie night. And in honor of your new project, I've found some they shot here in Cape May," Ben said. "Aunt Meg had a few on DVD, and that Vintage streaming service had a bunch of others. I thought it would be fun to see what the town was like back in the day—and maybe we'll pick up some ideas about the whole Regent thing."

"Can we have popcorn?" Erik teased.

"Of course."

"How about turning the lights off so we can make out like teenagers in the balcony?"

Ben's eyes went dark. "I think that can be arranged. Although it might cut down on what we actually see of the movie."

"That's just a risk we'll have to take." Erik gave him a grin that promised the best kind of distraction.

The spaghetti smelled fantastic, and Erik's stomach growled. "Everything looks great—thank you for putting all this together."

"Dig in," Ben replied. "I made plenty."

As they ate, Ben filled him in on the renovations to the rental units. Contractor delays, back-ordered materials, and other complications made for a frustrating day, although it sounded like everything had eventually been handled.

"How about you?" Ben asked.

Erik hesitated, not wanting to shift the mood. Ben reached out and took his hand.

"We're not strangers on a date," Ben said. "We're partners, and that means talking about what's going on, good or bad. You promised you wouldn't shut me out."

Erik managed a self-conscious smile and squeezed Ben's hand. "This part is new for me. Josh never wanted to 'talk shop,' and there were a lot of things I couldn't have told him even if he'd wanted to hear them."

"Caleb wasn't much for conversation either," Ben admitted, mentioning his former lover. "But we worked together, so he already knew the day job stuff. We never got past the 'first date' kind of conversation—movies, TV, sports. That's great, but not all the time. I always wanted to be able to just talk and not have to worry about every word."

"I think we can make that happen," Erik replied as Ben laced their fingers together.

"So?" Ben asked, raising an eyebrow.

Erik told him about going through the boxes. Ben paled when Erik mentioned the steel from the bombed car, recognizing the threat. He frowned with worry when Erik got to the part about his conversation with Alessia.

"Wow. That's some day."

"Yeah. Tell me about it." Erik pushed away his empty plate and took another sip of wine. "You and I never did figure out who killed Cafaro or why. I thought I could sense his ghost today, not up close but at a distance, like he still wanted answers."

"Having the ghost of a mobster hanging around isn't creepy at all," Ben said, rolling his eyes. "Monty's a medium. Maybe he can send Cafaro's ghost packing." Monty, the park ranger at the lighthouse, was a gifted spirit medium.

"Cafaro's not who I'd pick to hang out with, but I figure maybe I should keep him in sight—at least I know where he is." Erik wiped his mouth and leaned back in his chair, comfortably full.

"He's not here now." Ben glanced around in case he had missed something.

Erik shook his head. "No. Thank God. Maybe he knew he'd get an eyeful if he stuck around."

"I like the sound of that," Ben said with a grin. They worked together to clear the table and put leftovers away. Ben made popcorn, and Erik carried their drinks into the living room to settle on the couch in front of Ben's big TV.

"I thought we'd start with an adventure flick and then do a rom-com," Ben said as the first movie started. *Peril On the Waves* showed in the introduction, with a background of dramatic music.

"I wasn't expecting black and white," Erik mused.

"Looks like it wasn't long after the War," Ben agreed. "Color didn't go mainstream until the early Fifties."

"How'd you know that?" Erik asked, impressed.

"I looked it up when Sean and I did a marathon of old monster movies," Ben admitted.

They sat close enough to touch from shoulders to thighs, sharing the popcorn between them. Erik paid attention as the names flashed on the screen, recognizing Jason Corella, the leading man, and Peter Duncan, the producer, as well as Colette Dunbar—the starlet who disappeared from the Regent.

"All those folks came to a bad end," Erik observed.

"What about Robert Bowers, the director?

Erik shook his head. "I don't know. His name didn't come up. Worth looking into."

It didn't escape notice for either of them that both the Regent Theater and the Commodore Wilson Hotel managed to get their names into the opening credits.

Erik and Ben called out familiar landmarks like the lighthouse and some of the big Victorian homes and hotels. More things seemed to have stayed the same than Erik would have guessed. The plot itself was largely forgettable, a far-fetched action tale about an intrepid lighthouse keeper who singlehandedly prevented a Nazi submarine attack.

"The bunker looks so different," Ben said. The abandoned concrete military installation still stood on the beach not far from the Cape May Lighthouse.

"It used to be higher off the sand and a lot farther inland," Erik replied. "Shore erosion. They took the guns out in the late Forties. So when they 'fire' the artillery in the movie, that's got to be special effects."

"They did a good job with the explosions," Ben said. "Without computers, someone had to set off charges to make all the booms and bangs."

While the bunker's guns ultimately won the day by sinking the enemy sub, the handsome lighthouse keeper bravely fought off a Nazi spy, evading bullets, winning a hand-to-hand fight, and rappelling down the outside of the lighthouse in a move that had Erik's stomach in knots.

"There's no way the actor actually did all of that," Erik said. "I wonder who the stunt double was."

"It's probably in the final credits. The fight scenes are pretty decent. And lots of stuff blows up—also a point in its favor," Ben replied.

In the end, the lighthouse keeper not only sent the Nazis packing, saving the East Coast from invasion, but he also won the heart of a beautiful nurse. Erik and Ben watched closely as the final credits rolled, and Erik grabbed for paper and pen to make a note of a few more names, including Robert Bowers, the director.

"My grandmother would have called that a 'laundry' movie," Erik said as Ben went to refill their popcorn.

"Laundry?"

"Yeah. Good enough to pass the time while she folded laundry, but not needing close attention," Erik replied with a chuckle.

"She's not wrong. It wasn't horrible—although I don't think it took home any big awards."

"Filming movies here must have brought a lot of money into Cape May," Erik mused. "All the crew and cast members had to be here for months. They rented rooms, ate in the restaurants and bars, and bought stuff. And the movies brought in tourists who did the same things when they came to stay at the Commodore Wilson and see the movies at the Regent. Nice little racket."

"Until it all fell apart." Ben switched to the streaming service and selected a rom-com named *Of Sand and Stars*.

Erik recognized many of the background characters from the previous movie and wondered if they were local talent. Duncan had produced the film, and it had the same director—Robert Bowers. This time, he caught the name of the stunt coordinator, Jon Richards, in the credits. The leading man for the rom-com was the same as in the adventure flick, and the main actress was Colette Dunbar.

"Colette was sleeping with Cafaro," Erik observed. "And I think Jon Richards may have died at the lighthouse. Anna said a stuntman got killed there and might even still haunt the place."

"Oh yeah? The Cape May film industry sure had a high fatality rate," Ben replied. "What do you know about the main actor? He's easy on the eyes."

"He is, in a white-bread-kid-next-door kind of way," Erik agreed. "Corella is the guy I told you about who died in a car accident right after he'd had a fight with Duncan and made threats. They used the scenes he'd already shot for his next movie as a flashback in the new picture he was supposed to star in and wrote him out of the script."

Ben looked up. "Wow. That's not suspicious at all. And no one looked into the accident? The cops back then were either on the take or completely incompetent."

"Or intimidated into looking the other way," Erik added. "Some of the investigators I used to work with came under a lot of pressure to ignore 'inconvenient' evidence. I didn't envy them the choices they had to make."

They finished the popcorn and a second bottle of wine as they watched the comedy. When it ended, Ben looked to Erik. "Well?"

Erik stifled a yawn. "Fluffy, predictable—and fun in a cheesy sort of way."

"Yeah—not bad, considering. I've definitely seen worse."

They carried out the dishes and closed down for the night, then got ready for bed. Despite having looked forward to being with Ben all day, Erik could barely keep his eyes open. Ben slid beneath the covers, and Erik snuggled closer.

"I thought you'd already be asleep," Ben said in a fond tone. "You've been yawning since dinner."

"Sorry. I'm sure you could wake me up if you tried."

Ben leaned over and kissed him gently. "Oh, I've got plenty of ideas, but I'd have to stay awake, and I'm beat too. How about I set the alarm a little early, and we make the most of it?"

"Sounds like a plan," Erik replied, leaning up to brush Ben's lips with his own. They traded soft, sleepy kisses for a few moments, and then Ben lay down on his back, and Erik snuggled against him, loving how it felt to fall asleep in Ben's arms.

FIVE

BEN

B lowing each other in the shower more than made up for the night before and got the morning off to a grand beginning. The oversized shower was a definite benefit of his current apartment, and Ben wondered if Erik liked it well enough to consider moving in with him.

There's no big hurry. We'll figure it out.

Ben believed that, but he couldn't help thinking about taking the next step with Erik and making more of a commitment. With Erik being pulled in on Jaxon's project and Ben about to be hip-deep in renovating rental units, he figured this wasn't the best time to bring up a move. Still, he promised himself he wouldn't put off asking the question much longer. He suspected that Erik was also debating the best time to raise the issue. *Which one of us will blink first?*

He had picked up cinnamon rolls from Crumble's for a treat and set the coffeepot's timer before they went to bed, so breakfast didn't take long. Ben loved the stolen moments of quiet during mornings when they didn't have to rush because they'd planned ahead and could get the day off to a good start.

"Got plans today?" Erik dug into one of the pastries.

"I'm curious about the death of the stunt director since you mentioned it last night." Ben grabbed his coffee and sat across from Erik. "With your visions and Alessia's magic, you have much more direct ways to figure out what's going on with the curse, but a little regular investigating might turn up something interesting."

"Like what?

Ben shrugged. "It seems odd—especially if he didn't die in an on-set accident. Corella threatened to expose secrets. Duncan knew about Voorhis's murder. So what was the deal with Richards? Was he a witness to something? Did he know too much? And why did he die at the lighthouse? There's something not right—and it might tie in with the other Cafaro issues."

Erik frowned. "Let's hope that this time, we don't attract the attention of any living mobsters. I've got my hands full dealing with the dead ones."

They finished their sweet rolls, and Ben managed to talk himself out of a second. He saw Erik eyeing the box as well.

"Don't forget—we have dinner with Jaxon and Arjun tonight," Erik said.

"I'm looking forward to it."

Ben said goodbye to Erik at the door with a kiss and watched from the window until he was out of sight. With a sigh, Ben finished off his cup and poured the rest of the pot into a big travel mug, then headed over to the rental office.

Sorting out renovation details and complications took most of the morning, but by early afternoon things had slowed down enough so he could look into the stunt director's death.

The obituary and police report weren't hard to find. Jon Richards had been shot at close range by a large caliber handgun on the beach near the old bunker. The shooter had left him to die, apparently figuring he'd either bleed out or drown when the tide came in. Richards had managed to drag himself out of the water but hadn't made it to the lighthouse. The keeper told police he didn't see or hear anything. No suspects were identified, and no charges were filed.

Ben sat back and stared at his screen. The instincts that had made him a good detective screamed that something wasn't right.

Whoever shot Richards didn't make it a clean hit. So what was going on —and why was he there?

Unlike some of the others involved with the Regent's moviemaking, Richards had few mentions online. Ben found his birth records, driver's license, death certificate, and burial information, but little else. No marriage records or children, or even prior arrests.

"He just died and disappeared," Ben muttered.

Ben was about to give up when he ran the search a little differently and came up with a list of articles about the ghost of the Cape May Lighthouse—Jon Richards.

After he checked his email and phone messages for any urgent questions from contractors, Ben grabbed his keys and headed for the door. "If anyone needs me, have them call my cell," he told Jenny at the front desk. Ben grabbed a handful of real estate pamphlets as he passed the rack. "I'll be at the lighthouse."

Ben thought about calling Erik but remembered that Erik and Anna had more boxes to sort through.

The Cape May Lighthouse kept watch after more than a century and a half. Its white cylinder and red top made it a landmark for tourists, and the powerful light still guided ships at sea.

Tourist season was over, so the parking lot was nearly empty. Ben hoped the owners of the few cars remaining were out walking trails in the surrounding park so he could talk privately to the park ranger.

Montana Clark looked up when Ben opened the door to the small visitor's center. "Hey Monty! I brought you some brochures," Ben called out with a grin.

Monty unfolded his large frame from behind the desk. Ben wasn't a small man, but next to Monty, he felt tiny. Monty looked like a pro wrestler, with muscles filling out every inch of his six-foot-four frame. He kept his dark hair short during the summer, but when he let it grow longer for the winter and allowed his beard to fill in, he totally rocked the badass biker look.

"Thanks, Ben." Monty put the brochures into a rack next to the register, where tourists could buy snacks and souvenirs. "Don't know how many more visitors we'll get at this point in the year, but

I'm always happy to send them your way if they're looking for rentals."

"Much appreciated."

Monty waved Ben to a nearby chair and pulled up a seat for himself. "I don't think you drove out here just to hand me brochures. What's up?"

"Busted," Ben admitted cheerfully. He didn't know Monty well, but the few interactions they'd had went smoothly. Ben suspected that Monty liked the quiet and relative isolation that went with minding the lighthouse, but so far he hadn't gotten enough of the other man's story to know why.

"I'm looking for a ghost who's supposed to hang out near here. Guy named Jon Richards."

Monty stilled, and his eyes narrowed. If Ben ran into him on a dark night with that expression, he'd have hurriedly gone another way. "Who's asking?"

Monty almost seemed...protective. *Odd, since Richards died close to seventy years ago. Monty couldn't have known him...unless they met more recently?*

Ben had always been able to see ghosts, but unlike a true medium, he couldn't summon the spirits or channel them for a séance. Other aspects of the supernatural—like witches, curses, and Erik's touch magic—were new to him since his move to Cape May.

"Me. It might have something to do with a project, and I'm worried Erik and Jaxon are at risk."

Monty took a moment to consider his answer. "I know you're new in Cape May. There are a lot of ghosts here, but most of them don't bother anyone—and we don't try to make them leave. For a place as haunted as this town is, we've pretty much made our peace with having them around."

Ben nodded. "I don't want to hurt the ghost. If he's here and you can connect with him, it would help a lot to know what happened to him and what the connection might have been to the Regent Theater."

"Why?"

"Jaxon intends to renovate and rebuild the Regent. I'm worried that there are some loose ends that might send mobsters after us again."

Monty didn't say anything for a moment, and Ben worried that he was about to be thrown out. Finally, Monty drew in a breath and blew it out, then nodded.

"Jon says he'll talk to you."

"Has he been here the whole time?" Ben couldn't help looking around, but he didn't feel a spectral presence. That was unusual since Ben could usually sense when a ghost was nearby.

"Close enough," Monty replied.

"You know him? Or, I mean, his ghost?"

Monty nodded. "He sort of came with the lighthouse. When I started as the park ranger, I noticed him right away because he was a strong spirit and still had a sense of himself—he hadn't faded. He was used to hiding from ghost hunters because he wanted to be left alone. But I was here every day, and over time, we got to be friends."

Friends?

"He was lonely, and so was I," Monty replied, obviously picking up on Ben's unspoken question. "He started hanging out to watch TV with me, and sometimes I'd read a book out loud and he'd listen. Games too. He can flip playing cards for solitaire, roll dice, and play Shut-the-Box."

He's not kidding about them being friends. That's...interesting.

"How can I talk to him?" Ben couldn't help being curious. He'd seen carnival mystics who claimed to be able to contact the dead and always figured they were frauds. Erik vouched for Monty being the real deal.

"If it were a different ghost, the preparations would be a little more complicated," Monty said. "But since it's Jon and we understand each other, I just need a couple of minutes to center myself and for him to get into the right...vibration...for lack of a better term."

"Okay," Ben said. "Thank you."

Monty shook his head. "Don't thank me. It was Jon's decision. He has his reasons for wanting to talk to you. That doesn't guarantee you'll like his answers."

Ben waited silently while Monty closed his eyes and took several deep breaths. He didn't know what to expect. *Does this count as a séance? On TV, people have to sit around a table and hold hands. Can he channel Jon's ghost without all the trappings?*

Monty placed his hands flat on the table, fingers splayed. He squared his shoulders and breathed deeply. The room grew colder. Ben felt a shiver down his spine. Nothing had changed, but everything felt different.

The presence looking out from behind Monty's eyes wasn't Monty.

"I'm Jon." Monty spoke the words, but something fundamental had changed in his voice. "Ask what you want. I'll answer if I think you need to know."

Ben figured that anyone who had the brass balls to be a stunt coordinator would be a headstrong ghost. He reminded himself that the ghost's stubbornness probably contributed heavily to its "survival" after death.

"Why were you on the beach the night you died?"

Monty's head tilted as the ghost replied. "I was collecting from a dead drop at the old bunker. Cafaro's contacts would drop off either a bag filled with drugs or one stuffed full of money."

"What happened?"

Monty's expression grew pensive. "The guy I was double-crossing decided to double-cross me. I wanted out. That night, I picked up a duffel of money, and I was going to run away—get out of Cafaro's range. The bastard who made the drop shot me and left me to drown."

"Why were you Cafaro's errand boy? You were the movie stunt coordinator."

Monty's face twisted with the ghost's disgust. "Cafaro was a murdering son of a bitch. He killed Jason."

"Jason Corella?"

Anger faded from Monty's face, leaving grief in its stead. "Jason never knew when to keep his damn mouth shut." The desolation in his voice softened his words. "People treated him like he was an empty-headed idiot because he was beautiful, but Jason was smarter than most of the people around him."

Something in Jon/Monty's voice struck a nerve with Ben. He decided to run with his hunch. "Were you and Jason *together*?"

Monty paused again, longer this time, as he listened to Jon. "Yes," Jon said through him. "Monty has told me that things are not the way they were. Back then, we could have gone to prison for our love."

"Lots of actors were gay."

Monty shook his head, channeling Jon. "Not openly. They would have lost their contracts, been blackballed, never worked again even if they didn't go to jail. Jason was worth the risk." His voice had grown fond and wistful.

"Cafaro killed Jason—did he know about the two of you?"

"He found out somehow. We thought we'd been careful, but all it takes is one snitch with a grudge."

"Cafaro blackmailed you?"

"The only 'crime' I ever committed was loving Jason." Jon's bitterness came through clearly in Monty's voice. "Being Cafaro's errand boy put me on the hook for serious jail time if I'd been caught. That's why I was going to run."

"Do you have any idea who might have killed Cafaro—or wanted him dead?" The mobster's murder happened after Jon died, but Ben figured it was worth asking the question.

"Everyone?" Jon replied with a harsh laugh. "He wasn't on set much, but he'd call for meetings with the producer and director, and they'd come back plenty pissed. When he did show up, he swaggered around, making sure everyone knew he was the big cheese. Asshole."

Ben felt glad that after all the tragedy he'd endured, Jon had finally found a friend in Monty. Whether they were more than friends—or how exactly that might work—was none of his business, although Ben couldn't help being curious.

"We watched a couple of your movies last night," Ben said, figuring that since he had made the ghost relive sad memories, he could at least end with a compliment. "The one with the Nazi sub had some great special effects."

Monty brightened, still channeling Jon. "You liked that? Bob knew some guys from his Army days who set that up. They did all those shots. Looked pretty splashy on film."

"I'd better let you go," Ben said, knowing that allowing the spirit to speak through him tired Monty.

"You want my advice? Stay away from the Regent. It's bad news."

Monty slumped, and Ben's gift caught a glimpse of the ghost slipping away from the medium's body. Ben went to the fridge in the gift shop and grabbed a bottle of water, leaving a couple of dollars on the counter in payment. He pressed the bottle into Monty's hand and stood close in case he started to fall.

"I'm good," Monty assured Ben when he opened his eyes and nodded his thanks. He paused long enough to take a few gulps of water. "Jon goes easy on me. Who would he pal around with if he broke me?"

It sounded to Ben as if channeling Jon was routine for Monty, making him wonder once more about the nature of their relationship. He'd seen that old Patrick Swayze-Demi Moore movie; now he wondered if fact could be as strange as fiction.

"What about the lighthouse keeper who was on duty the night Jon died?" Ben asked once Monty had recovered. "Didn't he see anything?"

"After I got to know Jon, I went back and looked at the keeper's logs. We all keep a daily record that becomes part of the permanent history of the lighthouse. If the keeper saw anything, he didn't add it to the log. Maybe he thought it was more trouble than it was worth— or maybe the gossip is right, and he hit the sauce too hard and didn't notice."

From the police report, Ben knew the keeper hadn't reported finding Jon's body. That had been done by a couple taking a stroll on the beach. The interment had been in a local cemetery, although from what little Ben could find, Jon wasn't from Cape May. He wondered if the production company had made burial arrangements and if Jon had any family to notify.

"Thank you," Ben told Monty.

Monty finished his bottle of water and set it aside. "Jon and I aren't exactly *conventional*. But we're good together. He doesn't mind that I'm quiet, and I don't mind that he...has some challenges." He raised his chin, giving Ben a defiant glare as if daring him to make a remark.

Ben held up both hands in a gesture of surrender. "Hey, I'm not going to judge. If it works, I'm happy for you."

Monty held his gaze for a moment as if trying to decide if Ben meant what he said. His shoulders relaxed, and he gave a nod of acceptance. "Okay. Good. Thanks."

"Are there any other ghosts around the lighthouse that might have seen something that night?"

Monty shrugged. "If there were, I think Jon would have heard about it by now. There's a keeper from the 1890s whose ghost is pretty faded, and a guy who drowned back in the Seventies, also not a strong spirit. I'm not sure either of them is much more than a repeater—a memory loop without sentience."

He paused. "Look, I'd appreciate it if you didn't tell anyone about Jon and me. I'm not ashamed of us," he added quickly. "But I don't need people coming by to get a look or hassling us."

"Makes sense to me."

Ben might never say so out loud, but he thought the whole thing was sort of romantic. Most people wanted to find a "'til death do us part" relationship. Monty and Jon had something that transcended death. Ben knew his imagination would keep coming up with ways to make up for Jon's lack of a body when it came to sexy times, but he was totally okay with never finding out for sure.

Maybe Swayze got it right, after all.

———

"I love the way those pants fit your ass," Erik murmured as they walked up the wide driveway. Jaxon and Arjun's house was a beautifully renovated three-story Victorian with an ample backyard. The house was great for entertaining, capable of hosting large parties and numerous overnight guests without feeling crowded.

"Thanks. I like the way your hand fits my ass," Ben replied with a smirk. "You clean up nicely too."

Erik's tailored gray slacks fit his slim frame perfectly, and the midnight blue silk shirt played up his hair and eyes. Ben had opted for a light blue upscale island print shirt over black jeans. Jaxon had stressed that the evening was casual, but Ben knew that Jaxon's definition of the word didn't match what came to mind for most people.

"Welcome! Come on in, and you're a dear to bring wine. Right this way," Jaxon said, meeting them at the door. He wore Italian-made dark jeans and a simple linen shirt that Ben guessed was probably Tom Ford.

The whole house smelled of curry and garam masala, along with the scent of freshly-baked naan. While the outside of the house kept its traditional Victorian appearance, the inside had been completely remodeled, and Ben knew that the huge, professional kitchen was a point of pride for Arjun.

"Arjun is in the kitchen, putting the finishing touches on dinner," Jaxon confided. "He's been having a lot of fun—we haven't had guests in a while, so forgive him if he's cooked enough for a large Indian extended family."

Ben realized Jaxon wasn't kidding when they walked into the kitchen to find plates of samosas, a basket filled with naan, bowls of cumin rice, and several chafing dishes of delectable main dishes. Ben spotted palak paneer, tikka masala, something with lamb, and a few others he didn't recognize. A tray of desserts also caught his eye.

"Wow—you made all this? It looks fantastic and smells so good." Erik inhaled deeply.

"I'm saving room for dessert," Ben announced. "I know I liked what you made the last time, even if I don't remember what it was called."

"Ben, Erik—Welcome," Arjun Chandramohan said, his New Jersey accent as strong as ever. He wore a burgundy asymmetrical kurta over ivory-colored, slim-fitting churidar pants that flattered his build and played up his dark hair and eyes. Both he and Jaxon were barefoot, as were Ben and Erik, who left their shoes at the door. Ben had seen

Arjun in Armani suits for IPO announcements, in tuxedos for Arts Council fundraisers, and jeans and T-shirts at clam bakes on the beach. But he thought his host looked especially at ease in traditional comfort clothing.

"Thank you so much for having us," Erik said, handing off the bottle of wine to Jaxon. They knew they couldn't compete with Jaxon's wine cellar, so they chose an award-winning but affordable Verdelho that the man at the store swore was a perfect match for curry.

Jaxon went to open the wine and waved them toward the tall seats at the kitchen bar. "There are three kinds of pakora, plus some chaat to start with. Don't worry—everything will stay warm. Take your time. This is the perfect food for slow meals and long conversations."

Once they all had glasses of wine, Jaxon and Arjun settled onto stools on the other side of the bar where they could pick at the appetizers. Before Ben had gotten to know Arjun and Jaxon, he hadn't tried much Indian food. Now that he'd had Arjun's home cooking on several occasions, the newly familiar dishes had become favorites.

Arjun and Erik kept the others laughing with stories of travel mishaps from all over the world. Before Arjun retired from the software company he founded, he had apparently spent half his life on international flights, as had Erik. Jaxon's tales of Broadway foibles and behind-the-scenes mistakes were equally fascinating. Ben hung back, happy to let them share their stories.

"You're being quiet," Jaxon said, turning to Ben.

He shrugged, comfortable enough to admit the truth. "I was a Newark cop. It's not quite as exciting."

Erik elbowed him. "You have a lot of good stories. Like that naked rugby team? Or the burglar who got stuck hanging upside-down in the window?"

"You had me at naked rugby team." Jaxon grinned.

Ben's stories had Jaxon laughing hard enough to bring tears, and Arjun had to catch his breath. He recounted a couple more incidents and felt his confidence grow, surprised that stories about Newark's most clueless criminals could keep the others entertained.

They moved back to the main kitchen, where the candles beneath the chafing dishes kept everything hot. Ben and Erik filled their plates and followed the others to a table on the patio.

"This is all so good," Erik said in between bites. Arjun glowed with the praise, and Jaxon bumped his shoulder, a silent "I told you so."

"When I stepped back from running the company, I needed a hobby," Arjun said. Ben guessed that bringing the same focus to learning to cook that Arjun had used to create a successful firm and take it public translated into exceptional kitchen skills.

Jaxon went back to fetch a new bottle of wine. All through dinner, the four of them swapped stories, a friendly competition to find the most outrageous, unbelievable, and over-the-top tale. The desserts were just as good as Ben remembered, and he ate his fill with a silent promise to work in some extra exercise to atone.

Ben couldn't help watching how Jaxon and Arjun were together—so comfortable in their own skins and so in tune with each other. The frequent touches, brushing against each other when they moved, always in one another's space like a private gravitational pull.

They both seem so settled. I hope Erik and I can grow into that. I know it takes time, and I'm not trying to rush, but I really think he could be it for me.

"I know you've got other stories—ones that have to do with the Regent project," Jaxon said with a canny expression. "Now that you've been plied with all this food and drink—spill!"

Erik and Ben chuckled, although the information they had discovered was hardly funny. "You can *ply* us with your amazing cooking any time," Ben assured them. "But the stories aren't entertaining party conversation."

"With enough wine, anything is party conversation," Arjun assured them.

Ben and Erik exchanged a glance. No matter how they explained the situation, it was going to sound crazy. They took turns filling in what they had found out about the Cafaro connection, waiting until the end to bring up the curse.

"Voorhis, the guy who started the Regent, had a witch for a partner. They had a falling out. The partner put a curse on Voorhis—and on the theater—before he died," Erik said. "We're worried that might extend to Jaxon, with the Arts Council purchasing the theater."

To Ben's surprise, neither of their hosts laughed. Arjun gave Jaxon a pointed look, and Jaxon squirmed a bit in his chair.

"We'd heard about the curse," Jaxon said. "And you know theater people—we're superstitious. So I had heard that Voorhis was the target—but not the other version. After what happened the other day, maybe I shouldn't have been so quick to dismiss the stories."

Ben guessed from the look on Arjun's face that he had urged caution, and Jaxon had rushed ahead.

"We're just piecing it all together now," Erik replied. "Alessia is trying to figure out how the spell worked to see if we can break it. From what I can find, the effects hit different owners at different times. Faster, for the ones who kept the theater intact. Slower for the convenience store, although it seemed to finally catch up with them. Maybe it has something to do with keeping the building a performance space."

Jaxon paled. "I just signed the papers today."

"You think it will bring harm to Jaxon?" Arjun asked, anger barely covering fear. He reached for Jaxon's hand.

"It's possible," Ben replied. "We just don't know what makes the magic tick yet."

Jaxon shook his head and squeezed Arjun's hand. "There's no reason to think that a curse would jump to me. I'm not the owner of the Regent. The Arts Council owns it. I don't even own the Center for the Arts."

"We aren't sure the spell is going to understand that difference if you were the one who signed the papers," Erik explained. "Magic can be very literal."

"What can we do to keep him safe while you undo the magic?" Arjun's matter-of-fact question surprised Ben. Then again, as a programmer and a software designer, Arjun excelled at solving problems. It made sense that he would be less worried about how the dilemma happened and more focused on fixing it.

"Be careful," Erik said. "Try not to do anything risky. Just give us some time to figure this out. Alessia said she'd be willing to work some wardings on the house if you'd like and provide protective charms for you and Arjun. We aren't quite sure what we're dealing with yet, but I believe we'll get to the bottom of it."

Arjun got up and paced. "This is bad. Very bad."

Jaxon followed him. "Babe. It'll be okay."

Arjun turned, and his dark eyes flashed with anger. "You don't know that. I am not alright with risking you. Not for the theater, not for the Arts Center—not for anything. How can I protect you from something like this?"

Jaxon laid a hand on Arjun's shoulder, forcing the other man to look him in the eye. "I love you for wanting to, but you can't guarantee my safety."

"I will always try."

The other men weren't exactly arguing, but Ben felt uncomfortable witnessing the conversation. Erik put his hand on Ben's thigh, a welcome point of connection.

"Thank you for telling us." Jaxon turned away from Arjun as if he had suddenly remembered they had an audience. "I hope it turns out to be nothing. But given the history—I understand being careful."

As Ben had feared, the revelation dampened the mood. They lingered for a while longer, chatting about other topics, but the upbeat energy had shifted. Ben and Erik helped carry dishes to the kitchen, unsurprised when Arjun declined help with the cleanup. After thanking both their hosts profusely, Erik and Ben headed for the door.

"I'll walk you out," Jaxon said as they heard Arjun bustling in the kitchen.

"Everything was fantastic tonight. I'm sorry about the buzzkill at the end," Erik said as they walked down the driveway.

Jaxon shook his head. "Not your fault. I begged you to tell us." He glanced over his shoulder toward the house. "Arjun can be intense. He's very much about math and science and logic—but underneath that, he's all heart."

Jaxon shook his head. "My husband isn't religious, but his grandmother, who helped raise him, was quite observant. Curses are very serious things in the ancient stories, with dire consequences. I suspect some of those tales are coloring his reactions." He managed a smile that didn't quite reach his eyes. "I trust you to save my bacon. Keep me posted on what you find."

They promised that they would and waved goodbye as they pulled out of the driveway. The festive mood from earlier had dimmed, and Ben found himself just wanting to go home and wrap himself around Erik in bed, keeping them both safe and together.

Erik reached over and took his hand. "There's nothing else we can do tonight. Let it go for now. Alessia is going to call the coven together, and I'll email Simon and Teag to see if they know anything that would help."

Their friends had unique and arcane interests and abilities, valuable when dealing with supernatural dangers. Simon Kincaide's specialty was folklore, mythology, and the occult. Teag Logan was a hacker and a Weaver witch who had a network of friends with a variety of serious supernatural talents. "We're not in this alone."

Ben laced their fingers together. "I know. Sometimes it's just a lot. That's one of the many reasons I'm glad I have you."

They ended up at Erik's that night, as if both of them wanted the protection of the wardings. They crawled into bed, sidling close and holding on as if they might be swept apart.

"We'll get through this," Erik murmured, carding his fingers through Ben's hair. "And we'll figure out the rest. Together."

Ben held Erik tight, breathing in his scent, taking comfort from the strong arms around him. "I believe that. Together."

Erik's phone rang in the middle of the night. Both men woke, immediately on alert. Erik groped for his phone on the nightstand. He picked it up and put it on speaker.

"Arjun?"

"Jaxon collapsed not long after you left. We're at the hospital. I don't know what to do. The doctors can't figure out what's wrong with him, but he won't wake up."

"Did you call Alessia?" Erik got out of bed and shuffled around in the dark for his clothes.

"No. This is the first chance I've had to call anyone." Arjun sounded at wit's end, and Ben couldn't blame him, unable to even imagine how he would feel in the same situation. "Please...I need your help."

Erik knew that Arjun had faced down surly investors, cantankerous financial analysts, and recalcitrant boards of directors without blinking, but now he sounded lost and overwhelmed.

"We're on our way," Erik promised and wrote down the hospital and the room number. Ben grabbed his jeans and a T-shirt and was hopping around in the dark, trying to pull on socks.

"What do you think happened?" Ben asked.

"I think the curse happened," Erik replied. "It's awfully convenient to be a coincidence. Let's find out what's going on, and I'll call Alessia and put the word out to our friends."

Erik woke Alessia, who promised to come to the hospital. Then he left messages for Simon, Teag, and Sorren, asking for resources and whatever help they could offer.

He and Ben headed out in the pre-dawn dark, hoping that somehow they could solve the *strega's* curse and end the deaths—in time to save Jaxon.

SIX

ERIK

Erik hated hospitals. The antiseptic smell and washed-out fluorescent lighting triggered old memories of sitting at his grandmother's bedside in her last days and the days when he fought for life after being shot. Hurrying through the corridors to find Jaxon's room, Erik forced down his aversion and focused.

Arjun looked up when they entered. He had clearly pulled a few strings to get Ben and Erik in long after visiting hours ended. Arjun looked like he had aged a decade. His thick, dark hair was mussed like he'd been running his hands through it, and his eyes were haunted and worried.

"Thank you for coming." He rose to greet them. "I'm so scared."

Erik hugged Arjun. "Have the doctors said anything yet?" He glanced at Jaxon. Monitors hummed and beeped while IV lines and sensor leads threaded around Jaxon's chest and arms.

Arjun shook his head. "They did tests. The quick ones were inconclusive, and so I sit and wait for more results and watch him breathe." He moved back to Jaxon's bedside and took his husband's hand. "I don't think he knows I'm here."

"On some level, he knows," Ben assured him. "And talking to him, keeping physical contact, definitely helps. One of the guys on the force was in a coma after a bad fall, and they gave us a crash course on how to be a good visitor."

"Is it a coma?" Erik wondered how Jaxon could have gone from being so lively just a few hours ago to lying still and vulnerable.

Arjun shrugged and threw his hands up. "They don't know. We're waiting on test results and someone to read them, and meanwhile Jaxon is like this." He paced. "I called my brother in India. He's a neurologist. He's going to see what he can find. Our aunt has a *mantrik* she relies on for psychic readings who promised to help however he can. Beyond that…" Arjun spread his hands, palms up, in a gesture of helplessness.

"I called Alessia as soon as we got in the car. She's going to meet us here once she pulls together what she needs," Erik said.

Arjun's eyes were swollen and red from crying. "My aunt and my brother are the only family I have left. My father died years ago. My mother and the rest of my relatives were angry that I didn't accept an arranged marriage to the woman they wanted for me," Arjun said. "I married a man and someone who wasn't Indian. Most of my family cut me off."

"I'm sorry to hear that," Ben said. "Their loss."

"How can we help?" Erik asked. His parents had been as indifferent to his coming out as they had been to his entire existence.

"Just…stay for a while, if that's okay," Arjun said, squinting hard against threatening tears. "I know you've got work tomorrow. But it's too quiet here. *He's* too quiet. When has Jaxon ever been *quiet?*"

"We've got you," Ben assured him. He looked around. "Do you want coffee?"

Arjun looked relieved. "Please. I'm barely holding it together."

Ben nodded. "I'm an ex-cop. I can find coffee at a hospital like a dog on a fox hunt. Be right back." He headed out on a mission.

"I've pulled in some of our friends who know about these things," Erik told Arjun. "I can't guarantee anything, but if anyone can figure out what's going on, I think we've got the connections."

"Thank you." Arjun sat in the plastic chair beside Jaxon's bed. "I just...this is not something I can fix with an algorithm or throw money at. And it's *Jaxon*." He looked longingly at his husband. "My heart."

Erik felt his chest tighten. *Soulmates.* Erik hoped that he and Ben could forge that kind of connection, build on a good beginning, and create their own version of the bond he glimpsed between Arjun and Jaxon. *That's what I want. What I've always wanted. Someone who "gets" me for who I really am.*

His phone went off, sounding too loud in the hour of the wolf. "Alessia's here," he told Arjun. "How do we let them bring her up?"

"Tell her to check in at the front desk and say she's here for Jaxon," Arjun instructed. "I pulled a few strings."

Erik had never envied Arjun's wealth or Jaxon's fame. He was happy for his friends' success, but he had also been far too privy to the burdens that came with money and notoriety. While Jaxon and Arjun leveraged their name recognition for good causes, Erik's prior role dealing with some of the richest and most well-known people in Europe had shown him that money often brought a whole new level of problems.

Arjun turned back to Jaxon. He pulled his chair closer and laced their fingers together. "Did Jaxon ever tell you how we met?"

Erik thought for a moment. "I don't think so. Other than that according to him, you saw him perform, and it was love at first sight. I believe 'smitten' is the word he used."

Arjun gave a tired laugh. "That sounds like Jax. And he's right—I was thunderstruck. Gobsmacked. Twitterpated. I had gone to the theater alone since I had tickets and was between relationships, just expecting to pass a nice evening. And there Jaxon was, bigger than life, full of rage and passion and through it all—love. I was...transfixed," Arjun confessed.

"Oh yeah?"

Arjun managed to look a bit chagrined despite his clear wistfulness over the memory. "I had VIP seats. So I went to the concierge and bribed him to get me backstage. I was truly obsessed. Jaxon was alight in that part—incandescent. He lit up the stage—it was like no one else was even present. At least, for me. All I could see was him. I didn't know if anything might come of it, but I had to meet him. I had to let him know that I existed. I was like a man possessed."

Erik grinned, trying to picture his usually calm, cool, and collected friend so off his game.

"I was escorted backstage, and it was all so overwhelming," Arjun recalled. "I didn't know what to expect except that I had to see Jaxon. The concierge took me to Jaxon's dressing room, where he was hanging out with friends, sharing a bottle of champagne, relaxing. He was out of makeup, back in street clothes, and I thought he was the most beautiful man I had ever seen."

"So you swept him off his feet?"

Arjun gave a rueful chuckle and reached over to draw his fingertips lightly over his husband's cheek. "I wish. No. I stood there like an utter geek, completely tongue-tied. Me! I can talk angel investors out of millions of dollars and sweet-talk analysts into backing vaporware. But in front of Jaxon, I was completely undone."

"What did Jaxon do?" Erik asked, fascinated.

Arjun blushed. "Jaxon was in high spirits, fresh off a good night on stage, surrounded by his inner circle and toasting champagne. He looked me up and down and then met my gaze and stopped laughing, like what he saw startled him. Much later, he told me he saw his own soul looking back at him."

Despite his worry, a smile touched Arjun's lips. "He invited me to stay and asked me questions to draw me out. After a while, the others drifted away because all his attention was on me. I know it sounds rude, but Jaxon told me later that he didn't remember anyone else even being in the room."

"You make a great case for love at first sight," Erik replied.

Arjun's focus returned to Jaxon. "I can't lose him."

The door opened. Ben came in with a tray of coffee, and Alessia followed. Arjun rose and took Alessia's hand.

"Thank you so much for coming. It's an ungodly hour—"

Alessia shook her head. "It's alright. That's what friends do." She moved around Arjun to Jaxon's bedside as the others stepped back to give her room. Erik laid a hand on Arjun's shoulder while Ben set the tray with the coffee on a side table and came back to stand shoulder-to-shoulder with Erik.

Alessia held out her hand, fingers open and palm down, and let it hover from Jaxon's forehead down over his face, chest, and torso, then to his legs and feet. She kept her eyes shut, brows furrowed in concentration, lips pursed slightly with intense focus. Alessia stood completely still for several moments and then finally drew a deep breath and opened her eyes.

"What did you sense?" Arjun blurted.

Alessia turned to them. "Definitely magic. I can pick up on the shadows of old, dark power. Unless he makes a habit of pissing off witches, I think it's got to be from the theater curse. In fact, I'm almost positive—the energy signature is identical."

"Can you heal him?" Arjun's desperation was clear in his voice.

Alessia turned to him with a compassionate expression. "Not yet."

Arjun's face fell, and Erik tightened his grip, lending him strength. "Yet," he echoed. "Do you think—?"

"My coven is working to unsnarl the spell. It's old magic, and we think it's Russian—not something we've seen a lot of here. But one of my coven sisters knows a witch in Brighton Beach who studied the old ways. She's working with him to break the code. We put out a call to everyone we know in the community for help."

"I've got Simon and Teag digging into it, and they'll pull in Travis Dominick and his witchy Vatican connections," Erik added. "We'll find a way to fix this," he added and hoped his certainty wasn't misguided.

Arjun clenched his jaw. Erik realized that his friend was probably hoping Alessia could break the curse on sight. Just because such a hope was irrational didn't make it any less painful to be dashed.

"Thank you," Arjun said, his voice tight with emotion. "I am grateful to everyone for helping. Can you tell what the magic is doing to him?"

"I think it's a variation of a 'Sleeping Beauty' curse—named for the fairy tale, which would have gotten the idea from much older, darker folklore," Alessia replied. "Just like in the movie—only without the poisoned spinning wheel. The affected person goes into a deep sleep and doesn't wake up."

Erik frowned, already thinking of questions to ask when Arjun was out of earshot. *Why would the witch choose a slumber spell instead of a quick death? Is there significance? Some connection to the original falling-out with Voorhis? Maybe there's a clue in that.*

Back in the day, without modern medicine, a person hit by the curse would be dead in a week. We can keep coma patients alive indefinitely now... although that might not be a kindness. And is it a coma? She's carefully not using that word. Is Jaxon awake and trapped? Shit, that would be terrible.

"Talk to him, reassure him, let him know you're here," Alessia told Arjun. "If you want to try waking him with 'love's true kiss,' go ahead —but I don't think it'll be that easy."

Arjun looked crushed. "Is there nothing you can do?"

"Just because I don't have the answer right now doesn't mean we won't find one," she told him with a sad smile. "I don't think Jaxon is in pain. The hospital's treatments are keeping him safe while we work. We won't stop digging until we figure it out. In the meantime, you're going to have to keep the faith."

He nodded. "I will do that. Always." Arjun settled into a chair beside the bed. Ben put a cup of coffee on the table beside him and handed out the other cups.

"Do you need us to bring you anything from the house? Check on anything?" Erik offered.

Arjun shook his head. "Not right now, thanks. I have my gym bag and a change of clothes in the car—I was hoping that wouldn't be needed. I'll stay as long as they'll let me. But thanks."

"We'll swing by tomorrow but don't be afraid to ask if you want us to bring you food or anything else you need," Ben added. "And in the meantime, we'll work on getting rid of the curse. Just text us please if you get news from the doctors, and we'll let you know if we hit pay dirt."

"Thank you," Arjun said raggedly. "From both of us."

Erik and Ben walked Alessia to her car, even though Erik knew the witch could do much worse to any carjacker than turning him into a toad. "I got the feeling there was more you picked up that you might not have wanted to say in front of Arjun," Erik said.

Ben hung back, going into bodyguard mode so the others could talk without paying attention to their surroundings.

"Spite curses are hard," she said. "They're intended to be malicious and downright cruel. I'm fairly sure Jaxon is awake and aware, but he can't move."

"That would have been a death sentence back in the day." Erik's voice was hard and grim. "Except that in Voorhis's case, Cafaro murdered him before the spell kicked in."

"Exactly. Russian magic tends to be—no surprise—rather fatalistic. I think we need to look more closely at what befell each of the building's owners and look for patterns and variations," Alessia said. "And work those contacts. Someone somewhere has got to know something."

They waved goodbye as she drove off and then climbed into Erik's car for the drive home. Ben laid a hand on his thigh as Erik drove. "Fuck, I feel so bad for Arjun and Jaxon. I don't know how to deal with a threat I can't put a bullet in."

Erik had been mulling over the same thoughts, trying to imagine how he would cope if it were Ben cursed instead of Jaxon. None of the scenarios he came up with were remotely healthy coping mechanisms.

"I'll pump my contacts, and if you can get anything out of yours it's a plus. You're working with Brent Lawson and Austin Williams on that other project—surely three PIs with supernatural know-how can unearth something." Ben and the others were tracking down people who had "disappeared" from sanitariums in the Northeast during the past several decades who might have been shifters or clairvoyants. Erik knew the project was both tedious and often discouraging, despite its importance.

"You'd think," Ben muttered. "But I'll throw it out to the gang and see what comes back."

They tumbled into bed when they got home, barely bothering to strip off clothing. Erik figured they had a couple of hours left before the alarm went off, and he needed all the sleep he could get. Ben pulled him into his arms, and Erik fell asleep wrapped up in his lover, knowing both of them needed the reassurance that they were together and alive.

———

Breakfast was a hurried affair of grunts and grumbles, with both Erik and Ben barely awake. Even so, Erik didn't let Ben leave without a lingering kiss. "I love you," he murmured, holding on longer than necessary. Ben clung just as hard, and Erik felt sure they were both imagining being in Arjun and Jaxon's position.

"We'll make it better," Ben murmured, hesitating before letting go, as Erik buried his face in Ben's neck.

"I know we will. I just—"

"Yeah."

Erik headed to the store, unable to shake off his dark thoughts. *A friend is in critical condition, and another friend is totally losing his shit. That is a perfectly good reason to be in a lousy mood.* Still, Erik knew that he needed to function to be of any help to Jaxon and Arjun, and that meant getting his head into a better place.

Easier said than done.

Making a pot of coffee felt like a life-saving decision. Erik knew sleep deprivation would make the day hell and hoped that caffeine and sugar could offset the worst of the pain.

Susan arrived before the first pot had brewed. She took one look at Erik and her expression sobered. "Something happened. Tell me."

Erik gave her the short version, grateful he had a friend he could trust with the weird details. Susan listened, growing sad and angry by turns and ending with a thin-lipped look of determination that Erik knew meant trouble to whoever hurt someone Susan claimed as a friend.

"Anything I can do to help, just let me know. And if that means running the shop for a few days while you do the hocus-pocus needed to get Jaxon back on his feet, it's no problem. Is Arjun vegetarian? I make a great meatless white bean chili that keeps in the freezer. I'll put a batch in the slow cooker and drop it off with his housekeeper."

Erik's heart warmed at Susan's kindness and her take-charge mothering. "Thank you. I'm sure he would appreciate that." He knew firsthand just how good Susan's cooking was.

"That's what we do here in Cape May. We take care of our own," Susan replied as if it were the most natural thing in the world. From Erik's experience, that kind of compassion was far too rare.

Erik checked his email to see if any of the feelers he had sent out regarding Jaxon's situation had turned up helpful information. He'd received messages promising research and canvassing contacts, but nothing actionable. Frustrated, he headed into the break room, where two new boxes of memorabilia awaited.

Anna hadn't arrived yet, but Erik didn't mind starting without her since he knew he needed to adjust his mood to be fit for company. He approached the boxes carefully, starting with an outside scan so he could anticipate any dangerous or powerful objects.

The first box gave off the jangled energy Erik associated with strong emotional resonance—not necessarily haunted, but possibly trouble. There was definitely *something* going on with at least one item inside. The second box, to his relief, didn't register any strangeness, so he pushed it over toward where Anna would sit and carefully dug into the first box.

The items were old props from films shot in Cape May, donated by people who had worked on the movies—or their heirs—and the studio props department. Nostalgic but otherwise worthless stuff left over from movies no one remembered.

Erik couldn't deny feeling a little star-struck fascination as he pulled out the pieces. Some were signed photographs, while others were trinkets probably purloined by actors and crew as mementos—costume jewelry, knickknacks from sets, and stage weapons that looked good but didn't work. Thankfully, an inventory described each item, its donor, and the movie it came from, sometimes even detailing the actor or scene where it appeared.

He spotted a fake handgun that the roster said had been used by Jon Richards, Monty's ghostly lover, in one of the movies Erik and Ben had just watched. Ben had told him about Monty and Jon, and while Erik was still wrapping his mind around their connection, he wished them well. He took a picture of the prop and resolved to let Monty know when it came up for auction, in case Jon cared.

Handling the other pieces made Erik even more curious to watch the old flicks, and he hoped Ben would be up to the challenge. If Jaxon could pull off a retro film festival as part of his grand plan, Erik bet it would be a big success since the movies, while dated, were good enough to remain entertaining.

So far, none of the pieces had stirred more than a minor tingle of psychic energy, which was to be expected from heirlooms and collectibles. But as he neared the bottom of the box, the burn of a strong resonance made him recoil.

A small item wrapped in tissue paper nestled inside a plastic bag, accompanied by a note. As soon as Erik touched the bag, the strength of the emotional resonance hit him hard enough to make him slide from his chair to the floor.

He saw a handsome, dark-haired man in his early thirties, dressed in black, with an intense expression. Another good-looking man came into view, and Erik recognized Voorhis from old photographs. He couldn't hear the conversation between the two men, but the sexual tension was unmistakable. Voorhis flirted shamelessly, clearly captivating the younger man.

Erik recognized more images as being the interior of the Regent Theater. At first, the two men were obviously in accord—and perhaps more than just associates. Then he saw Voorhis with his arm around a pretty starlet and glimpsed a screaming fight between Voorhis and the other man. More images gave Erik the impression Voorhis made a habit of being seen with the leading ladies of Cape May's films. The dark-haired man brooded in the background with what Erik could only read as jealousy.

Time jumped, and the next scene made Erik a witness to a brutal shouting match between Voorhis and the other man. When the younger man turned his back, Voorhis drew a gun and shot without hesitation. Erik saw shock and betrayal in the dying man's expression, but when his lips began to move, Erik felt a chill as if the dark magic could reach him through the vision. As his heartbeat slowed, the man clenched his fist around a locket that hung from a chain around his neck.

Voorhis left, then returned with a tarp. He laid it on the floor and rolled the man's body onto it, roughly enough that the locket pulled free from the chain, still gripped in the dying man's hand. When he had concealed the body, Voorhis lifted it in his arms, face empty of emotion. Erik couldn't hear the words Voorhis spoke, but he thought he could read the man's lips. "Land-fill." Erik saw a flash of gold as something—probably the locket—fell to the ground.

"Are you okay?" Anna knelt beside Erik, where he lay on his back on the floor. His heart still pounded from what he had seen as his mind rushed to make sense of the images. The bag with the tissue-wrapped object lay near his right hand.

"Yeah. I will be," Erik replied, chagrined that he had fallen from his chair. "Would you mind picking that up, please? What's inside is important—but I don't want to handle it."

Anna lifted the bag gingerly, but it clearly had no effect on her. Susan waited until Erik was back in his seat at the table before she brought him a fresh cup of coffee. They listened intently as he told them what he had seen.

"Open it," he said to Anna. "Let's see what the note says."

Anna laid the bag on the table and withdrew the wrapped item, winding back the layers of paper to reveal an engraved locket. She unfolded the note and began to read.

"My name is Alan Saunders, and I used to work at the convenience store that was in the lobby of the old Regent Theater. When I found a door that led into the auditorium, I would sneak off and explore. The old place wasn't in quite so bad shape back then."

Anna frowned as if deciphering the handwriting, then went on. "One day, I got brave enough to check out some rooms on the second floor. One of them looked like it had been a small apartment, and I poked around, wondering if whoever lived there had left anything behind. I found this under the radiator.

"I know I shouldn't have taken it, but at the time it didn't seem like the theater belonged to anyone. I kept the locket safe all these years, but I feel like it wants to come home now that you're bringing the theater back to life. I hope you can use it in your exhibit."

She held up the locket so they could see it in the light. Erik stared at the elaborate etching.

"Can you turn it so I can see the front, please?" He leaned in, squinting to make out the detail. "There's a monogram hidden in the design. 'B&T.'"

Erik looked up, eyes widening as he realized the significance. 'Benjamin & Thomas.'"

Susan had a puzzled expression. "Why would Voorhis give his witch a necklace…oh."

Erik nodded. "Yeah. From what I saw, I'd say it's a pretty sure thing that Voorhis had an affair with Ruccio, which they would have had to keep secret. Voorhis didn't seem too invested, but I'm going to bet that Ruccio was in love with him. Voorhis played the field, and Ruccio got jealous. Then Ruccio got in the way, and Voorhis shot him. Ruccio didn't just curse his murderer—he put a spell on the lover who betrayed him."

Anna's eyes were wide. "Wow. You put a whole new spin on 'bringing history to life.'"

She reached for the box, and Erik blocked her before she could pull it closer.

"There's something else inside that's got bad juju," he warned. "Better let me handle it."

"Wouldn't it be better to have one of us do it?" Susan asked. "We won't be affected like you are."

Erik shook his head. "Just give me a few minutes for the coffee to hit and my head to clear. I'll be fine."

Susan and Anna chatted about Yoga class and the upcoming concert in the park while Erik gathered his wits. The bell in the front of the store chimed as someone entered, and Susan excused herself to deal with the customer. Erik finished his drink and set the cup aside.

"We don't have to do this right now," Anna told him, worried. "It can wait until tomorrow."

Erik's intuition warned against delay. "I have a hunch that whatever's inside is important. If it knocks me for a loop, maybe this time I won't fall off my chair," he said with a wan smile.

Carefully, he reached inside the box and pulled out an object swathed in bubble wrap. His heartbeat sped as he clipped away the tape that held the wrapping in place and carefully released the item from its protections. Erik gasped when he saw what was inside.

The porcelain figurine had the sleek lines of Art Deco styling. Erik recalled this particular statuette from his days tracking down art thieves. Its theft had made international headlines at the time, but the piece had never been found—until now.

Erik knew the vision was coming before it overtook him, giving him enough warning to rest his hands and the precious figurine on the table. *Images flashed in his mind. He saw a woman in a sleek 1920s-era gown, the piece's original owner. Other images showed parties and a glamorous mansion. Then darkness and rough whispers, and the figurine passed through various hands, hurried and furtive.*

Distant voices mumbled, and the figurine was moved again, surrounded by an aura of fear and greed. It came to rest in a new place, still shrouded in darkness, a hoarded treasure. He felt a web of emotions from the thief—fear of discovery, vindictiveness in the choice to steal the piece, satisfaction at having gotten away with the theft, and a clear, recent level of malice that made Erik's blood run cold.

"Erik?" Anna called, sounding worried. He shook his head to clear it and took a deep breath.

"Sorry—the figurine packs a wallop," he replied.

"What did you see?" Susan and Anna almost spoke in unison. Susan stood in the doorway, and Erik realized that he had been distracted long enough for the customer to have come and gone.

Erik weighed how much to tell them and decided to stick to the truth. "There was a similar statuette in one of the Cape May movies

Ben and I watched. But this one was a custom commission for Odette Landon. She was an actress who married a wealthy New York financier, and the figurine was made to resemble her. As I recall, she and her husband were big names in Cape May at the time. When she died, the estate sale listed the statuette for an astronomical price.

"Then someone pulled off the biggest art theft in New York history, and the Landon figurine—along with several other expensive pieces—vanished," Erik concluded.

"You look like you've seen a ghost," Anna said.

"This piece shouldn't be here. It's the real thing—priceless and hot as hell."

Anna leaned over his shoulder to peer at the figurine. "Hot as in sexy or—"

Erik shook his head. "Stolen hot. By the Russian Mob, we thought, although we couldn't ever find enough evidence to charge anyone—or get the items back."

"Russian Mob?" Susan's eyebrows rose.

"One of my first major art theft cases," Erik said as he carefully examined the piece to confirm that he hadn't lost his mind. "Nothing says 'welcome to the big time' like annoying mobsters."

"Then how did it end up here?"

"Good question. It's not haunted or cursed—but it's far too valuable to be lying around, and technically, it's evidence in a cold case crime," Erik replied, wracking his brain to figure out who among his old contacts he should alert.

"Did someone steal it from the Mob?" Anna's eyes were wide. "That would take brass balls."

"Oh, there were plenty of thieves with those," Erik replied with a rueful chuckle. "But what stumped us was that the thieves had buyers lined up in advance, so when we tracked them, the goods were already gone, and we couldn't prove the guys in the warehouse were involved without the stolen pieces. They were pros."

"Maybe someone donated it out of guilt?" Susan suggested from the doorway where she could hear their conversation and still keep an eye on the front door.

"Hell of a donation," Erik replied. "The heist was front-page news for a while, and this was one of the items whose photos were splashed all over the papers and the internet. Between the fame of the maker, the custom commission for a celebrity, and the notoriety of the theft, the provenance alone puts this in the low seven-figures—and bidding would drive that up even higher."

Susan let out an appreciative whistle. "Damn."

Anna dug out the inventory list and looked up the number on the statue's tag. "Big surprise—the donor is listed as 'anonymous.'"

Erik stared at the porcelain figure as if it might bite. "So we have no way of knowing whether the piece was intentionally donated for some weird sort of atonement—or something else."

Anna and Susan both spoke at once. "Like what?"

Erik shrugged. "No way to tell. Whoever bought it from the guys who stole it had Mob connections. Normally, that kind of item either stays in a family as a secret treasure or is sold discreetly in a private transaction."

He scrubbed a hand down over his face as the ramifications became clear. "Having a missing treasure surface like this will make the news. That could potentially expose the donor and raise uncomfortable questions about his or her circle of friends. It adds a hint of scandal to the exhibition that will make an even bigger story. But having it land in my lap definitely exposes me."

Erik carefully wrapped the figurine and put it in the safe, grateful when no other images forced themselves on his mind. Only then did he realize how hard his hands were shaking. Susan pressed a hot cup of coffee into his grip and steered him back to his chair.

"That's why you turned down the TV show they wanted you to do, isn't it?" Susan said, and Erik guessed she was mentally putting the pieces together from conversations earlier in the season.

Erik took a gulp of the java and then nodded. "Yeah. Having the shop and the online store-slash-blog keeps the focus on the unique curios we sell, with some history and art background thrown in. The TV show would have put me on camera, talking about the cold cases and the stolen art that 'got away.' Might as well have put a target on my back."

"Target?" Anna echoed, horrified.

"I helped international law enforcement bust bad guys. I was the expert witness at their trials. Made more enemies than friends. And now that I'm out of the game, retirement didn't come with a bodyguard detail."

"You've got Ben," Susan replied.

Erik winced. "The last thing I want is to put him in harm's way."

"Don't you think you should leave that up to him?" Susan asked.

Erik sighed and then hid behind his mug for a few sips. "Oh, I'm sure that's how it'll turn out. And I know he'd do it willingly. But I didn't come here to bring trouble with me. I thought I was out."

"So did Ben," Susan said. "Different mobsters, same long memories. Kinda like what Al Pacino's character said in that Mafia movie about how every time he tried to leave—"

"They dragged him back in," Erik finished. He rubbed his eyes with the heels of his hands. "Fuck. I really didn't need this. The exhibit doesn't need this. Jaxon—shit, I need to see if anyone's gotten back to me about him."

Anna looked up, startled. "Jaxon?"

Erik didn't want to give away confidences, but he had to say something. "He got sick suddenly, and we think it might have a paranormal cause. We're trying to find out how to fix that."

He got up and pulled his phone from his pocket. "Anna—I'm sorry. Everything else in my box checks out as 'supernaturally safe.' You brought plenty of coffee and fresh donuts. Please, continue without me. I need to give Ben a head's up and then see if I can help with Jaxon's situation."

Erik went back to the privacy of his apartment and listened to his voice mails, then called Ben. "Hey," he said, hoping he didn't sound as rattled as he felt.

"What's wrong?" Ben's concern told Erik his acting skills needed improvement. "Is Jaxon worse?"

Erik slumped into a chair in the living room. "I haven't heard anything new about Jaxon—or gotten tips from anyone I put out the word to. But we might have a problem—"

"Are you hurt?"

"No." *Not yet.* "I think someone is trying to out me to the Russian Mob."

"Fuck."

"Yeah." Erik told him about the figurine and its history. "I haven't called my old contacts yet, but I'll need to before long, or holding onto it will look suspicious. But the heist was so famous, with lots of juicy scandal, that it will make the news when the piece surfaces again. And even if my contact promises to keep my name out of it—"

"Once it comes up linked to Cape May, you're easy to find," Ben finished, voice tight. He paused. "So...how do you want to handle this?"

"Susan promised to give Chief Hendricks a head's up since he's coming over to her house for dinner tonight." It was occasionally awkward and also convenient that Susan's son was the Cape May police chief. "I'm sure that will endear me to him," Erik added in a wry tone. "I'd ask if you could trace who sent the item, but I honestly have no idea where to start."

"Do you have the package it came in?" Ben asked. "Even if the Arts Council threw away the wrapper, they probably have some kind of spreadsheet to log in the memorabilia as it arrived. It's worth a shot to ask."

"I'll call Tess. She's Jaxon's assistant."

"Is the figurine something the Mob would come after you for?" Ben asked.

"Not the statue itself. There were a lot of cases, and I helped to put dangerous people behind bars. The kind of people who hold grudges."

Erik knew Ben understood. The fear of retaliation hung over every cop, no matter the level of the agency they worked for. Ben had made his own share of enemies in Newark, both in the Mob and with other gangs and criminals. Cape May felt like a world apart, but with highways and airports, the past was far too close.

"Brent and Austin were able to find some leads on Voorhis's witch, and I sent that intel on to Alessia," Ben reported. "They're also helping figure out the missing pieces of the Cafaro story. With the theater coming back to prominence, I have a feeling that could bite us in the ass if we don't know who set up his murder."

"Travis said he had some ideas he wanted to look up in that secret Sinistram library," Erik replied. "And he said he had an in with a bunch of Polish Orthodox priest/demon hunters who might know something about Russian witches. He has Alessia's number, and he'll call her when he knows more. Teag's shaking down all his witchy contacts, and he promised to call Alessia directly, so that takes me out of the middle."

"Just another day in paradise," Ben muttered.

"Let's get dinner at The Spike. Now that the tourists have gone home, we might even score a chair by the fire pit," Erik said.

"I like that. After we swing by and check on Jaxon and Arjun," Ben said.

"It's a plan."

Erik ended the call and then placed another to Tess. He told her that one of the donated items was exceptionally valuable and wanted to know who the donor was so the Arts Council could properly thank them—and explore the provenance.

Tess had been happy to check their records, confirming that a ledger did exist, logging all the donated memorabilia in as much detail as possible. She promised to be back with an answer as soon as her next meeting was over, which still left Erik with several hours to wait.

He pulled up his contact list, knowing he couldn't avoid the inevitable. Erik hadn't gotten around to purging the names and numbers from his old life, perhaps because deep down he wondered if he would ever need them again.

He scrolled, mentally putting faces with names. Some people he remembered positively and others not so much. He came to the contact he had been looking for and hesitated, staring at the screen as he sorted through an avalanche of conflicting emotions.

Finally, he pressed *call*. A familiar voice answered. "You've reached Timothy Long. Please leave a message."

Erik had chosen Tim's personal phone because he didn't want to explain himself to the gatekeepers who managed the official line. They had worked closely—and urgently—enough to trade personal numbers, although the relationship between them had always only been professional.

"Tim—it's Erik Mitchell. The original Landon figurine just showed up on my doorstep—literally. It's authentic. I don't know what the hell to do with it, so I'm calling you. Tag—you're 'it.'"

He hadn't talked to Tim since a few months before he'd left his old job. Since Erik had worked with a variety of law enforcement agencies in the US and internationally, his "boss" on any particular case was the ranking agent or officer in charge. Some he worked with more often than others, and a few he'd been glad to leave behind. Tim was one of the good ones.

Erik paused to pour himself a glass of milk and eat a muffin, stalling before going downstairs and plunging back into the boxes. He didn't expect to hear back from Tim until after the workday ended, and maybe not for a couple of days if Tim was out on a case.

When his phone rang, Erik was so surprised he nearly dropped his muffin.

"Erik? Good to hear from you. How the hell are you?" Tim's Carolina drawl made Erik smile.

"Great to hear from you too. I'm doing well. How 'bout you?"

"Eh, you know how it is. The crazy never ends. I've switched agencies to another set of initials since you left—doing the same sort of thing. Are you making a go of being out?"

"Yeah," Erik replied. "Believe it or not—I am. Things are good. I get shot at less, although that number still isn't zero yet. I keep getting pulled into cold cases involving dead mobsters and live shooters."

"Sounds like you," Tim agreed. "So—the Landon figurine? Fuck! How—"

Given the high-profile item and the nature of the situation, Erik felt certain that despite Tim's folksy welcome, their call was recorded, and he spoke accordingly.

"A local arts group is remodeling a big classic theater that had Mob ties back in the day and doing a splashy exhibit about the theater's history to help raise funds. I got pulled in to authenticate and triage a bunch of old movie-related memorabilia," he told Tim.

"I was going through a big box of stuff, and there's the figurine. I knew they'd used something similar in one of the movies shot here, but Tim—this is definitely the real deal. All the telltale identifiers are there. The details are right. Since it was donated to the Arts Center project, whoever's had it all these years ceded their rights to it, and I guess it belongs to the Center. It's a mess, Tim."

Erik paused, surprised that he felt nervous enough to want to be sick, just from thinking about being back in his old job.

"We'll need to do some legal mumbo jumbo to figure out who owns what," Tim replied. "If it was donated, then at least the Arts Center didn't buy it at auction, so they won't be out any money if we have to seize it. You know that's probably what's going to happen." He paused. "So how did you end up with it?"

"Like I said, I was helping them go through the donated memorabilia to sort the good stuff from the junk, and there it was—all done up in bubble wrap and as pretty as ever, no worse for the wear."

"Where is it now?"

"Secure—somewhere else," Erik said, unwilling to go on record with the location. He wanted to think he could still trust Tim—at one time, he wouldn't have doubted it for a moment, and he'd have been right. But that was then. *And this is now*, his inner voice commented. *You're not part of the team anymore. Loyalties can shift.*

"Are you sure? There's a lot riding on not losing that damned piece again."

"I'm sure. How and when do you want to send someone to get it?" Erik asked.

"Can you bring it to us? I'm in downtown DC these days."

Erik's intuition jangled, part experience and part mojo. It had never been wrong, and he had ignored it at his peril. Now, that sixth sense told him not to go to Washington.

"I don't feel safe transporting the item," Erik replied, figuring that was a reasonable deflection. "It's a lot more secure where it is now than in my car. Don't you have some agents in the area who can swing by? I can take them to it."

The slight hesitation before Tim answered made Erik's gut clench. *What the fuck? Does he suspect me somehow? If I'd been involved with stealing it all those years ago and gotten away with it, why would I let it surface now? Or is this part of a bigger cat-and-mouse game?*

"I'll see who I have in the area," Tim said smoothly, and if Erik hadn't played the game for so long he might not have noticed. "Guess I was just hoping we could catch up on things if you made the trip."

They had worked well together at the time, but they had never been buddies off the job. Usually Erik had stayed in his hotel room alone while the Feds did whatever they did after hours. The loneliness was as bad as the danger and constant travel, one more reason he was glad to have left that life behind.

"I traded all that glamor and excitement for a quiet little resort town," Erik said, keeping his tone light. "Not much to tell."

Not exactly the truth, but Tim wouldn't understand the supernatural side of things. Erik had learned that the less said the better.

"I'll send someone your way in a couple of days," Tim replied. "Text me your address. I presume you haven't forgotten how to check to make sure the person with the badge is legit?"

"I got shot—I didn't hit my head," Erik said in a droll tone. "Yeah, I remember."

"Great. This will help us put a bow on that old case. I'll be in touch."

Tim ended the call. Erik didn't move, replaying the conversation in his mind. *Did I somehow become a suspect, or has Tim just gotten more paranoid?*

He struggled to remember whether he had told Tim about buying Trinkets and doubted it had come up. They hadn't had any reason to talk once the case wrapped up. Getting shot took Erik off the board early, and the rest of the team handled tying up loose ends—all except for the Landon figurine.

Is he going to think it's suspicious that I bought a store that deals in antiques and curios? It's not like I opened a high-end auction house. But will he wonder if I've become a fence?

Erik shook his head, wondering if he was the paranoid one. *I'm jumping to conclusions. Tim might just have been distracted.* But that didn't explain his gut feeling that something was wrong.

With a sigh, Erik pocketed his phone and finished his coffee, then headed downstairs. He ordered a pizza for lunch, which Susan and Anna helped finish in no time. Anna had made good progress on the second box, and Erik enjoyed combing through the pieces she unwrapped, all of which were utterly mundane.

He picked up a glossy photo and realized it was a behind-the-scenes shot of an action sequence being filmed. Erik recognized Jason Corella, the star, and squinted for a better look at another man who seemed vaguely familiar.

"That's Jon Richards, the lead stuntman and stunt coordinator," Anna said, and Erik's eyes widened as he remembered what Ben had told him about meeting Richards's ghost at the lighthouse. "He died tragically—something of a scandal at the time. Such a shame—he had a lot of talent."

Even more of a tragedy than anyone knew. Knowing that Cafaro's threats to "out" Richards and destroy him had led to the stuntman's desperate attempt to escape saddened Erik and made him grateful to be alive at a time when he and Ben could live openly and marry for love.

That's jumping ahead a bit, but I think with Ben it could work. I thought about it with Caleb, but it never felt right. Ben and I haven't been together all that long, but it feels like we've known each other forever. Thinking of making it official doesn't scare the shit out of me or make me nauseous. I'm grateful that we have the chance.

"Ben and I watched some of the movies. Considering the budgets and the level of special effects at the time, they did a remarkably good job," Erik said, hoping to cover zoning out.

The rest of the items in Anna's box were posters, scripts, lighthouse souvenirs, and promotional pieces for movies that included the Commodore Wilson monogram. "I think these will work well in the displays Jaxon has planned," Erik remarked. "Did you have a chance to look at the things I laid out?"

Anna nodded. "None of them were as fancy as what you found before, but maybe that's a good thing. There were some nice photos of Cape May at the time, pictures from fancy premieres at the Regent, more stuff from the Commodore Wilson. Good, solid background."

Erik shrugged. "That's important for the history side of the exhibit. The flashy stuff gets attention, but the details tell the real story."

They finished going through the memorabilia before closing time, and Anna took the boxes back to the Arts Center, promising to bring new ones in the morning.

His phone buzzed, and he saw Tess's name flash on the display before he accepted the call. "Hey, Tess."

"Hi, Erik. I've got the information you wanted. It's not much. A last name, an address—that's it. Sometimes people include a note about how they got the item or why it was important to them, but there's nothing recorded for this one."

"Can you please text me that name and address? A gift this generous should be recognized, and I'm intrigued to find out how they came to have the piece." Erik stuck as close to the truth as possible.

"Sure. Anything else?"

"The gift piece looks a lot like a prop that was used in a couple of the movies, but there are important differences. Can you see if you can find photos of the mantle over the fireplace in the Ellsworth house in *Moon Over Cape May?*"

Tess chuckled. "That's oddly specific, but I'll give it a shot. When I find something, I'll let you know."

He thanked her and ended the call.

"Good news?" Susan asked, hopeful.

"Maybe. Tess has a name and address for the donor. I'll see what Ben can dig up about them. The big question is—how did they get the piece in the first place?"

Susan laid a hand on his arm. "Don't worry too far in advance. Things have a way of working out."

Erik hoped with all his heart that she was right, but experience had proven time and again that "working out" often came with a hefty cost.

Susan was in a hurry to get dinner started for her son's visit, and Erik looked forward to getting some downtime. He locked up carefully and then resolved to push his worries out of mind for a few hours so he could enjoy the evening with Ben.

SEVEN

ERIK

E rik and Ben went to the hospital together. Arjun welcomed them, and he managed a tired smile at the sandwich and coffee they brought. The bag of books they handed off made Arjun tear up.

"Thank you," Arjun said. Day-old scruff and his haunted gaze made him barely recognizable. "It's been a long day. The books will help pass the time. There's not much on TV."

"Did the doctors have anything to say?" Erik asked.

Arjun returned to his seat near Jaxon's bed and put the food bag on the tray table. Jaxon lay too still and pale, with wires and tubes running everywhere. For someone who was always in motion and larger than life, the contrast was jarring.

"The doctors don't know," Arjun said. "That's what it all boils down to. Even my cousin, the neurologist couldn't say. Nothing fits the usual diagnoses for the symptoms, and they're stumped."

"Because it's magical," Erik replied.

Arjun looked completely wrecked, going on far too little sleep. "That appears to be the best guess, but not something the doctors will believe."

He carded his fingers through his dark hair. "They can't explain the sudden onset or the way his brain is active like he's awake. But at least they can keep him alive until we find an answer and make sure he's not in pain."

Arjun winced at that last comment and tightened his left-handed grip on Jaxon's hand. "I've explained it all to him. So if he's awake, he knows what's going on. I've begged him to hang on and fight, to stay with me. But where does that leave him? If we can't find a cure—"

"We're not giving up—and neither should you," Ben said. "Erik and I are both working our contacts, and that's a pretty big network of people who know a lot about the supernatural. We're profiling the witch who cast the curse right now."

Ben laid a hand on Arjun's shoulder. "I swear to you—we'll figure this out."

Arjun hung his head. "Thank you," he said in a broken voice. "That means the world to me."

They stayed for a while, chatting about the news and odd incidents in their days. Erik told him about the latest two boxes—except for the problem figurine—while Ben made snarky comments about delays in renovating his company's rental units.

"Is there anything we can do?" Erik asked.

Arjun raised his head and looked straight into Erik's gaze. "Protect each other. This isn't over."

Erik raised an eyebrow. Arjun had never admitted to any psychic abilities. But then again, as a high-profile entrepreneur, he was more in the spotlight than anyone else—with more to lose and more reasons to keep such things hidden.

"Can we sit with Jaxon while you take a break?" Erik asked. "We'll completely bore Jaxon telling him what we did today, but that lets you get some fresh air and a change in scenery."

Before Arjun could object, Ben jumped in. "You're no good to Jaxon if you burn out. You've got to pace yourself."

"Word's gotten around the arts community," Arjun said. "Tess is putting a schedule together for people who want to stop in to read to him or bring meals once Jaxon goes home. I appreciate it."

Erik nodded. "Alessia is making good progress figuring out the Russian magic behind all of this."

Arjun turned away. " I keep hoping that this is a bad dream. But I don't wake up."

"We'll save him," Ben assured the other man. "We've got the best people working on it. Jaxon's safe for now. We'll bring him home."

———

The Spike was a local landmark, a Cape May presence for more than fifty years. Its menu served up comfort food for breakfast, lunch, dinner, and late-night, with a casual dining room inside and a very popular outdoor bar. The seating area included fire pits, Adirondack chairs, and Cornhole games. A small stage showcased live music on weekends. Once the tourists left and the place wasn't mobbed, The Spike had the kind of charm that made everyone feel at home.

Erik veered off to use the restroom and then wound through the crowd to catch up. He spotted Ben at the bar and sidled up beside him.

"Waiting for someone?" he asked as if he was flirting with a stranger. He and Ben had met for the first time right here, a case of mistaken identity when Ben turned out not to be the guy Erik had picked from a dating app. Despite the mistake, they had still managed to find each other, for which Erik was amazed and grateful.

"Matter of fact, I am." Ben gave Erik the once-over like he had never seen him before. "He looks a lot like you, in fact."

Erik stepped closer into Ben's space. "That so? Can I buy you a drink while you wait?" he asked, going along with the role play.

"Hmm. I guess so. But I'll warn you—he's the jealous type." Ben's eyes flashed with heat and humor, sending a rush of warmth straight to Erik's cock.

"Enough already, you two!" The bartender gave them both a look. "You're so damn cute together I can feel my teeth rot." Her smile softened the comment. Sherry Weller owned The Spike with her wife, Jo, and had made it into a vital part of the year-round Cape May community.

Erik dropped the teasing and took the stool next to Ben, still sitting close enough that their shoulders bumped and their knees touched. He ordered the same thing Ben drank, a locally-brewed seasonal lager, and only took a moment to glance at the familiar menu before ordering a Reuben, while Ben got a bacon cheeseburger.

"I'm really glad your date didn't work out that night," Ben said, grinning at Erik as the band came back from break and started to play a mix of yacht rock and beach favorites.

"Me too," Erik replied, still thrilled at his good luck in finding Ben.

"I can't believe you thought I was with Sean. He's my cousin, for fucks' sake!"

Erik shrugged, palms up. "How was I to know that? He's a good-looking guy, and he had his arm around your shoulder like he belonged there."

"That's just Sean. He's done that since we were kids. For being a big jock, he puts himself out there with his heart on his sleeve. If he considers you to be family—blood relation or otherwise—he loses all concept of personal space," Ben replied. "And don't ever tell him he's good-looking. His head's big enough as it is."

Erik knew that Sean was the closest thing Ben had to a brother, and he certainly didn't begrudge the relationship. Ben's father was long gone, and he and his mother had been estranged since his teen years when she demanded he go into the priesthood and refused to believe he was gay.

His aunt and uncle here in Cape May had taken Ben in, put him to work in the rental business, and provided the support Ben had needed to get through that period until he was old enough to go to the police academy in Newark. Sean, their son, was part of the package, and Ben always said that their escapades were some of his best memories.

They ate quickly then took a new round of drinks to sit by the fire pit. Erik basked in the luxury of doing nothing, staring into the flames and letting his mind go blank.

"You okay?" Ben gently elbowed Erik.

"Yeah. Just worried about Jaxon and weirded out about the 'item' that showed up out of the blue."

Ben reached over to take his hand. "We'll work it out," he promised.

Erik managed a smile. "I know. And I believe we'll figure out how to help Jaxon. But a phone call didn't go the way I expected, and I'm not sure what to make of that."

He didn't want to spoil the mood, and discussing the details of his call with Tim in public was out of the question. Ben squeezed his hand.

"Can you let it go for a couple of hours? I think we could both use a break."

"I'm sorry," Erik said. "I get like this. If you hadn't noticed."

Ben met his gaze. "Your focus is your superpower. But it's okay to turn it off sometimes, so you can rest."

"I'm still learning how to do that, but I want to improve," Erik confessed.

"Not my strong point either, but that's okay. Just stare at the fire, drink your beer, and breathe."

Erik focused on the dancing flames, on how solid and anchoring Ben's grip was on his hand, at the background hum of conversation and music, and the salty caress of a late-summer ocean breeze. Deep breaths helped Erik center himself, something he'd learned from the mandated psychologist when he was recovering from being shot. He wondered if Ben's level-headed wisdom came from a similar source when he had been recuperating from the shootout that helped to end his police career.

God, what a pair we make. His-and-his matching gunshot scars.

"I want to get a tattoo."

Ben's head swiveled, and his eyes widened. "Come again?"

Erik couldn't resist a smirk. "Always for you, sweetie."

Ben shot him a sultry smile. "I know you will. But I meant—what did you say?"

"I want to get a tattoo," Erik replied, surprised at the sudden certainty.

"Okay." Ben drew out the word, skeptical. "Of what?"

"*Nec metu*," Erik said as the phrase came to mind without needing to even consider. "It's Latin for 'without fear.'"

Ben shook his head fondly. "That's my geek boy. Why the sudden urge to get ink?"

"Tats are hot."

Ben's color rose to Erik's amusement. "Did Sherrie slip some vodka in your lager?"

Despite Ben's comment, Erik could see that his partner preened at the compliment. If Erik was being completely honest, he had something of an obsession with Ben's tats. He loved to trace the tribal markings with his tongue, and the *non timebo mala* over Ben's scars fascinated Erik.

"I thought I'd have it done over the scar," he said, feeling suddenly bashful. "Doesn't Sean have a friend who's a crazy-good inker? Maybe we could take a road trip to Wildwood and get him to do it."

"You do know that it hurts?"

Erik had figured as much. He also hated needles. But he'd been thinking of a tattoo for a while now. He wondered if while he was at it, Alessia could recommend a protective sigil they could both etch into their skin to ward off evil.

Soulmates, Erik thought. With all that term implied, matching ink seemed trivial.

"That sounds great," Ben replied with sincere enthusiasm. "Sean's friend does amazing work. You'd be happy with it." He paused. "I think it would be hot. Although…it seems sort of sudden."

Erik shrugged. "I didn't know I had a 'thing' for tattoos until I saw yours. I feel a little plain."

Ben met his gaze. "You're perfect just the way you are. Do it or don't do it—but make sure it's what you really want. I'm totally okay either way."

"Thank you." Erik felt a little overwhelmed. The day had been full of whiplash emotions, and everything seemed to crash down on him at once. He upended his bottle, finishing the lager. Ben seemed to pick up on his intentions.

"Ready to head home?" Erik couldn't put into words why he felt like it was essential to be back in their space, but he felt that pull in his marrow.

"Sure," Ben said, not seeming as surprised about the sudden shift as Erik expected. Erik felt a flash of guilt for pulling them away from the fire and the band. Ben turned toward him as if he could read Erik's mind.

"It's completely okay," Ben assured him. "You had a rough day. This was fun, but I'm ready to go back."

For a moment, Erik thought Ben was going to say "home," and his heart leapt in his chest. *Home. Wherever Ben is. Together.*

"There was a time when I would have closed this place," Erik said wistfully.

"We still could," Ben replied. "But I've got other things I'd rather do." The look in his eyes gave Erik an instant semi.

"I like how you think," Erik replied with a smile that promised everything.

They'd already paid their tab. Erik listened to the strains of music until they faded in the night, drowned out by distance and the roar of the ocean.

"Thanks," he said. "I needed that."

"I enjoyed it too," Ben said. "It was nice to get away from thinking about things for a while."

"Whose place?" Erik asked.

Ben gave him an assessing look. "Yours. It's safer."

"I'd like something to be ours." Maybe it was the lager or the moonlight. Erik couldn't help blurting out what he felt and then held his breath for Ben's reaction.

"I'd like that too," Ben confessed. "But first, we've got to get you through this figurine and movie mess. I'm not going anywhere." He tightened his grip on Erik's hand as they walked. "We have time."

"Thank you." Erik struggled to deal with all the conflicting emotions. The call with Tim worried him, because he was concerned that his former protector might now see him as complicit.

Russian mobsters, Jaxon and Arjun, witches. Am I going to get rendi-tioned to Gitmo over a stupid statue? And showing up like it did—is someone out to get me? Am I putting Ben in danger? Did Tim go rogue, and is he part of the problem?

"Stop that."

"Huh?'

Ben glared at him. "Oh my God. I'm not even psychic, and you're thinking so loud you're gonna give me a headache. Enough with the blame already. What happened to Jaxon is *not your fault.* Figuring this out is not all on your shoulders. And I'm a big boy. I can take care of myself—and you."

Erik pulled him close and kissed him, just a quick brush against his lips—acknowledging, thanking, promising.

Erik let them into the apartment over the shop, and they stripped off clothing as soon as the door latched behind them. He let himself get lost in slow, tender love making. Erik tried to focus on the here-and-now, on the weight of Ben's body in his arms, the warmth of his lover's skin, his scent and taste.

"So good for me," Ben crooned, stroking Erik's hair and sliding his hands down Erik's back. "Just happy touching you, if that's all you want. Love having my hands all over you. Fuck, I'm addicted to you—and I love it," Ben breathed.

Erik reached between them, wrapping his fingers around both their cocks. Ben grabbed lube from the nightstand and drizzled it over Erik's palm, easing the slide against each other. He wrapped his hand around Erik's, making a warm, slick channel for them to fuck into as they continued to kiss and mouth at each other, more about comfort and satisfaction than urgent climax.

Erik came first, with a moan instead of a shout. Ben crested a moment later, covering both their hands with their release.

"Feel better?" Ben asked, sliding the fingers of his clean hand through Erik's hair.

Sated and a little buzzed by the high of orgasm, Erik nodded and nuzzled against Ben's neck. He licked at the hollow of Ben's throat, liking the salty taste of his sweat, and breathed deep, taking in his partner's scent and the smell of sex. He was starting to doze when the rumble of Ben's chuckle roused him.

"Unless you want to stick together—not in a good way—I need to get a washcloth."

Erik bit back a noise of protest as Ben extricated himself from the tangle of limbs and padded to the bathroom, returning in a few moments with a warm washcloth and a hand towel. He gently wiped away the jizz on Erik's stomach and hand, then moved lower and dried off the wet spot on the sheet with the towel. He tossed the cloths toward the door and slid under the sheet with Erik, who rolled on his side to splay his hand on Ben's chest.

"Love you," Erik murmured, half asleep. He heard Ben's reply echo his sentiment just before he drifted off.

The cavernous warehouse looked like a set out of a low-budget horror movie. Exposed pipes and conduit snaked across the ceiling, while rows of crates cast long shadows beneath the pale, insufficient fluorescent lights.

Nothing about this meet-up felt right, and Erik had to consciously stop himself from fidgeting. His Interpol handler assured him they had agents in place for his protection and that once Erik confirmed the authenticity of the stolen artifact, the backup would swoop in and get him out of there.

As soon as his contact arrived, Erik knew his cover had somehow been blown. Even before the mobster opened his mouth, everything about the man had gone from congenial to sharp-edged.

Erik stuck with his role, tried to play his part as fear and desperation twisted in his gut and bile rose in his throat. The glint of malicious humor in the Russian's eyes confirmed that he was toying with Erik, waiting to pounce and make the kill. Backup might come, but they would be too late.

Erik saw his contact pull a gun. Pain tore through him, and blood flowed warm and sticky over his hands where he clutched his belly.

Then the lights went out, except for one bare bulb. Men screamed. Something that wasn't human moved like a blur, evading bullets and ripping the heads off the mobsters. Impossibly strong hands grabbed Erik, carrying him like he weighed no more than a child. The last thing Erik remembered was the blast and heat as the warehouse exploded.

The scene changed from past to premonition. Instead of waking up in a hospital in Antwerp like the real memory, Erik found himself in Ben's bed at the rental apartment in Cape May. Erik's hands patted down his stomach and found no blood, no raw wound. Just a long-healed scar.

Breathing a sigh of relief, Erik headed to the kitchen, lured by the smell of coffee and bacon. Ben stood at the stove, shirtless and in sleep pants and an apron, looking more delicious than the food smelled. Erik's morning wood took notice.

He was just about to sidle up next to Ben when the outside door slammed open. Heavily armed men in ski masks pushed their way inside.

"Erik Mitchell. Come with us," one of the men said in a heavy Russian accent.

Out of the corner of his eye, Erik saw Ben go for the handgun he kept in a kitchen drawer.

A gunshot rang out, deafeningly loud. Ben's apron blossomed red, and he stared wide-eyed as his knees buckled.

"Ben!" Erik couldn't breathe, and he moved to go to his lover.

"Leave him. You're coming with us," the shooter said.

Erik fixed the man with a defiant look and ran to Ben's side, cradling him in his arms. "So, shoot me. You're going to do it eventually. I'm not leaving him." He pressed his hand over Ben's wound, sick as warm blood covered his palm.

Ben's breath came short and fast, and he was far too pale. Erik wrapped his arms tightly around him, defying the intruders or Death itself to separate them. "Together," he whispered, pressing his lips against the side of Ben's head. "Forever."

The crack of the second gunshot woke Erik, who roused flailing, unable to process the fact that they were safe in bed.

"Whoa! Slow down, take it easy," Ben coaxed, sleepy and worried.

Erik couldn't hear over the pounding of his pulse and his harsh, panting breaths. He grabbed Ben by the shoulders, panicked. "You're alive." He patted down Ben's torso and then pressed a hand against his own belly, finding both of them unmarked.

"I'm okay," Ben assured him, no doubt guessing the turn Erik's dreams had taken by his desperate triage. "You're okay. We're safe."

Erik's ears buzzed, and he felt lightheaded from the pounding of his heart. "Safe?"

Ben nodded. Erik searched his gaze and found no judgment. "Safe. Bad dream?"

Erik wiped a hand across his face, unsurprised it came away wet with sweat and tears. "Yeah. Combination of what actually happened and what I hope never does."

Ben squeezed his shoulders and kissed the top of his head. "I have nightmares too. Goes with the territory."

"I guess." Erik struggled to pull deep, even breaths and tried to calm his pounding heart. Ben was right here, alive and well. And as far as Erik knew, the Russians hadn't found him yet. "I don't want you to get hurt." Erik couldn't help flashing on memories of his twisted dreams.

"I'll be okay. We'll deal with it."

Erik knew that Ben wasn't psychic. He hadn't seen Erik's dreams, where the past cost him everything he wanted for his future.

"How—"

Ben cupped Erik's cheek and stared into his eyes. "Because I know the man I love. I believe in him. And I trust him with my life—and with the world."

EIGHT

BEN

E rik's nightmare rattled Ben more than he wanted to let on. They both had their share of bad dreams, times when the real and imagined near-misses loomed large, and all of the alternative possibilities became real.

Ben knew Erik was freaked out about the Russian Mob connection, fearing that enemies from the past had found him and might uproot his new life. Ben had a stake in Erik's future, and he wanted to make sure it included Cape May and him. He was determined to fight to make that happen.

Ben told Jenny that he wasn't to be disturbed, took a big cup of coffee into his office, and shut the door. He'd managed to get enough details out of Erik about the figurine to do some digging through his private investigator resources. Ben knew that Erik could be badass when the chips were down. But now it was time for Ben to prove he was a worthy partner and do his part to protect his lover.

He started with the address Erik had gotten from the Arts Council for the donor of the figurine. Ben searched the databases patiently, tracking names and real estate sales, drivers' licenses, public records, and social media.

Ben pivoted from one database to another, patiently working the process. He read everything he could find about the history of the stolen figurine. Regular media alleged Mob ties. Reports that were only available to people with the right credentials went into much more detail about the Russians, money laundering, and the bigger picture as it related to global crime.

He lost track of time reading and then searched specialty law enforcement databases for Erik's name, coming to realize that his boyfriend had played a bigger role in several major busts than Erik ever let on.

The accounts were sobering, not just for the danger Erik had faced but also for the high profile crimes he'd been part of busting. Paris, Mumbai, Abu Dhabi, Singapore, Berlin, London—Erik had traveled the world helping find stolen artwork, identify fakes, return relics to their rightful owners, and stop antiquities theft.

Ben's world seemed small by comparison. He'd been to the Canadian side of Niagara Falls and went to Cancun once for vacation, the total extent of his world travel. Erik had been able to fit in among art enthusiasts and celebrities. *He's out of my league.*

Another mental voice stepped in to argue. *He chose me. I choose him. That's all that matters.*

The deeper Ben dug into his research, and the more he learned about Erik's past, the clearer it became that Erik would never be completely safe anywhere, short of going into WITSEC. If it came to that, Ben was prepared to go with Erik, whatever it took. But he knew from his own dealings with Mob informants that even the US Marshals couldn't guarantee an asset's safety.

Still, it's safer with two. Ben wasn't ready to tell Erik yet, wasn't sure Erik was ready to hear his decision, but he'd already made up his mind that Erik was it for him. Alessia's revelation about them being soulmates had validated something Ben felt deep in his marrow. Maybe his soul called to Erik's soul. Ben left it to the priests and dreamers to figure those things out.

What he knew in his bones was that he and Erik were supposed to be a team, partners in every way. They were still getting comfortable with one another and with the intensity of their bond, and Ben was content to take their time—unless Erik's safety was at risk. Ben already knew he would do anything—*anything*—to protect Erik. The certainty scared him a little, even as it warmed his heart.

All the more reason not to worry him about the Newark Mob angle until I'm sure it's worth the effort, Ben told himself. He rationalized that he wasn't withholding information—just not mentioning what might turn out to be a baseless hunch, saving them all needless drama.

His conscience pinged him, a reminder that regardless of the rationale, he was being less than honest with Erik.

I'll tell him—if it turns out to be anything important. There's no need to worry him on top of everything else until I know for sure.

Ben wasn't surprised to find that the name and address provided to the Arts Council by the figurine donor were fake. But as an investigator, he knew people rarely pulled false identities out of thin air. There was nearly always some kind of connection, and if he could figure out the link, he could find the person who sent the statuette.

He went out to refill his mug and check in with Jenny, then returned to his desk. TV made private investigators look glamorous, but ninety-nine percent of the work was a determined slog through public records.

Ben ran through the history of the house at that street address and searched for anyone with a similar last name. A flash of inspiration made him decide to check not just the usual civilian resources but also a database of known Mob associates, focusing on those with ties to the faction suspected in the original heist.

While the searches ran, Ben checked email, answered calls from contractors with questions about the unit renovations, and drummed his fingers impatiently. He jumped when his phone rang, surprised to see it was from his cousin, Sean.

"Hey! What's up? How's the food truck biz treating you?" Ben remembered his sense that Sean had been a little off during their last call and hoped whatever the problem was, it had turned out okay.

"I need advice." Sean usually embodied Jersey Boy confidence, the blue-collar swagger that epitomized Garden State icons like Springsteen and Bon Jovi. Ben knew it was mostly a front and that underneath the fun-loving, bad boy persona, Sean was far more intelligent, well-read, and sensitive than he let on to anyone outside his inner circle.

Now, Sean sounded rattled and scared.

"Are you in trouble?" Ben checked his watch. He could be in Wildwood in half an hour, maybe a little more if he had to navigate around road construction.

"Someone's shaking down the food trucks for protection money," Sean blurted. "A big guy with no neck and a Russian accent made the rounds of all the trucks last night with a version of, 'nice set-up you have—be a shame if anything happened to it.' He gave us until tomorrow to come up with five grand each. *For now.* Or else bad things happen to us and our rigs."

"Fuck," Ben muttered.

"Benny, I'm scared. The truck is making a profit, but I don't have money like that just lying around. Everything I've got goes into supplies and maintenance. And if I pay up, what's to say it won't be more next time?"

"It will be. Count on it. Those SOBs don't care if they bleed you dry," Ben muttered. His computer pinged to let him know the searches were done, but right now, his attention was on Sean.

"I talked to the other truck owners. Some of them are going to bite the bullet and pay. The rest are split between going to the cops or sticking together and refusing. I don't know what to do."

"Bring your truck here," Ben told him, not needing to think about it. "We'll hide it, you can stay in one of the units, and we'll figure things out. Do not try to be a hero. Those guys want an excuse to make an example of someone and scare the shit out of the others. This is a fight you can't win—at least, not head-on."

"Okay." Sean sounded like a scared kid.

"Once you're safe, we'll come up with a plan—and decide how much you can trust the local cops. How soon can you leave?"

"It's the last day of a gig for a big beach volleyball tournament. I'd rather not cut and run since it could turn into a yearly thing, and we've made good money from it. The event wraps at five."

Ben fretted over the delay, but he understood Sean's reluctance to burn a bridge with a good customer in case they could find a way out of this mess. "Okay. Don't tell anyone where you're going or when you'll be back. Don't do anything out of the ordinary—act like it's just another day. Leave as soon as you can."

"I've got to say something to the guys at the apartment, or they'll worry and file a missing person's report." Sean's three roommates were his best friends. Ben knew Sean couldn't just disappear on them.

"Tell them someone tried to shake you down and that you're going to lie low for a few days," Ben said. "That way, they know to be extra careful and not let anything slip if anyone comes around looking for you. They'll probably guess where you'll go, but it's safer for them and you if they don't know for sure."

"That works." Sean's voice sounded higher pitched and breathier than usual, which told Ben his cousin was terrified.

"Call me when you get to Cape May. Do you remember the big garage behind the rental duplex out near the lighthouse? The one your mom and dad always kept for people who needed to store an RV or a boat while they were here?"

"Yeah. I know where it is."

"No one's using it right now, and there's plenty of room for the truck. I'll meet you there."

"Okay." Sean related the word like a mantra as if he was trying to stave off a panic attack. "Thanks, man. I knew you'd know what to do."

"I'll remember you said that," Ben teased, trying to lighten the mood. "I so rarely get accused of being a good influence."

"You're the best," Sean replied, and Ben knew his cousin was really spooked to let his usual bravado slip.

"I've got your back," Ben said. "Just get here safely and make sure you aren't followed. Be careful."

Sean promised and ended the call. Ben tried to pull his thoughts together. He knew he couldn't have turned Sean away, but Ben also realized that he'd given the Russian Mob one more reason to come to Cape May, exposing Erik to more danger.

"Shit," he muttered, knowing it was a no-win situation. He turned his attention back to the computer and started through the search results. Ben wasn't entirely sure what he was looking for, but he knew he would recognize it when he saw it.

An hour later, a name popped up that wasn't on the donor form, and neither was the address. But it turned out to be an alias of a mobster, a known associate of the man suspected of masterminding the figurine theft. Ben felt sure that he'd found the right person.

Jack Donahue was the name on the apartment lease—one of more than a dozen aliases for Joakim Denikin, a guy with such a long rap sheet, Ben didn't think he had enough paper to print it out. Denikin had been picked up on a slew of minor offenses, done brief stints in prison, but always managed to avoid having major charges stick.

That told Ben that Denikin's boss considered him valuable enough to bother pulling strings to keep him from serving serious time. Ben had seen plenty of betrayals among career criminals, but he'd also seen surprising loyalty. Smart crime bosses nurtured that loyalty by being generous with favors, helping the families of their most valued lieutenants, binding those associates to them with indebtedness.

The saps didn't realize until too late that when the chips were down, loyalty only ran one way.

Ben glanced at the time. While he had a couple of hours before Sean arrived, he had no intention of showing up alone and unprepared to confront a goon who was undoubtedly well-armed and nursing a major grudge.

That might be proof I've gained some alleged maturity.

Trying to collar Denikin by himself was a bad idea, but he *could* run down some questions he had about the Newark Mob connection to Cafaro's still-unsolved death. That meant going back to the lighthouse and seeing if Monty and Jon Richards's ghost would be willing to humor him. Between the Regent's renovation and the *strega's* curse on Jaxon, Ben felt certain that this nightmare wouldn't be over until they got to the bottom of the long-ago murder.

Besides, the garage for Seth's truck is near there. It's on the way.

He saved the results of his searches and backed up the files so he could access them from both his home computer and his phone. Ben asked Jenny to close up and headed for the lighthouse. He tamped down his worry about Sean, much as he forced himself not to obsess about the dangers to Erik and Jaxon.

Ben called Erik as soon as he got into his car and gave him a quick recap of Sean's dilemma and that he'd made progress on finding the person who sent the stolen figurine.

"Please don't go after him alone," Erik begged. "Turn it over to Chief Hendricks. Whoever sent it has ties to people who won't hesitate to kill anyone in their way. Nothing is worth putting you at risk."

Except keeping them from hurting you, Ben thought. "Bringing Sean here might draw attention from the Russian goons who tried to shake him down. I didn't know what else to do—he needed to be safe, but I didn't want to put you in more danger."

"You did the right thing," Erik said without hesitating. "Bring him to my place. Both of you should stay with me until this blows over. Safer together."

"Thanks," Ben said, letting out a breath he hadn't realized he was holding, afraid of Erik's reaction.

"Of course." Erik paused. "Alessia and I are working with Travis Dominick and some of Teag Logan's friends in Charleston on the *strega* curse. I think we're close to cracking it, so I'm going to be late. We'll probably order pizza and work through dinner."

"I'm expecting a personal visit from a food truck full of gourmet onion rings," Ben replied. "I doubt I'll starve. It'll take a while for Sean to get here and square away the truck, so we won't be at the apartment anytime soon. Just...call me if you decide to work through the night, so I don't worry."

"I promise. I'd rather be wrapped up with you in our bed," Erik said. "Love you. Please, Ben, be careful."

"I promise. Love you back. And being careful goes for you as well." Ben ended the call, unable to rid himself of a jangly feeling of apprehension.

He pulled into the lighthouse's nearly empty parking lot and stared up at the tower that wasn't just a landmark and a piece of local history

—it had become an iconic image defining Cape May. The white cylinder had been built to withstand the strongest hurricanes, and the red top made it easily recognizable. Its powerful light blinked every fifteen seconds, still a beacon to ships finding their way.

Before he went to see Monty—and hopefully, Jon—Ben decided to take another look at the old bunker. He couldn't define what fascinated him, but the attraction felt undeniable. Maybe it was just the existence of a "secret" hideout or the allure of an abandoned bolthole. The boxy, concrete fortification hunkered on the sand, much closer to the waves than when it was built, stripped of the sod that once disguised it.

The guns had been removed long before Ben was born. Signs warned away trespassers. Wooden barriers covered locked steel doors. Ben had read everything he could find on the bunker. With walls of six-foot thick, reinforced concrete, and guns that could fire shells at ships miles out at sea, the bunker must have seemed invincible. The twenty rooms inside contained crew quarters as well as generators, a water purification system, a switchboard, and an airlock in case of chemical warfare.

Designed to be a last outpost on the coast.

He circled the bunker slowly, thinking about Jon being black-mailed into being Cafaro's courier. The area around the bunker was deserted, and Ben shivered, thinking about approaching the hulking fortress in the dark. While it now belonged to the state park, back when Cafaro used it as his drop site, the bunker had still been military property.

Cafaro had brass balls, that's for sure.

Instinct made Ben pivot seconds before something swung at his head, and he barely avoided the strike. Ben's training kicked in, letting him react without the need to think. He dodged another blow from what looked like a riot baton and plowed into his attacker's stomach, taking them both to the sand.

He couldn't get a good look at his attacker in the fading afternoon light. Ben regretted not carrying his gun—an oversight he intended to rectify if he survived.

The stranger clipped Ben on the temple with the butt of his baton, and Ben reeled, giving way just enough for the assailant to twist out of his grip and struggle to his feet in the shifting sand. He swung the baton at Ben two-handed. Ben rolled away, barely evading the strike, and kicked his attacker in the knee—then threw a handful of sand in the man's face. Ben thought the man looked vaguely familiar, and the green stripes on the man's jacket sleeve stuck in his mind.

The man cursed and swung again as Ben lost his footing and staggered. He braced himself for a skull-cracking hit, managing to turn to take the brunt of the blow on his shoulder, painful enough to make his vision blur. Ben knew that he would die if he went down, but he couldn't keep his footing.

The temperature plummeted, going from cool to frigid in seconds. Mist formed between one breath and the next, and a man's form took shape, gray and nearly solid, standing between Ben and his attacker.

The stranger yelped, startled, then turned and ran. Monty was already on his way, changing course to pursue the attacker while the ghost remained with Ben. Ben staggered back toward the lighthouse. Before he had gotten halfway, he saw Monty running toward him. The lighthouse keeper was a mountain of a man with an unmistakable silhouette.

"Ben! Hang on, I'm coming." Monty reached him seconds later and got under one shoulder, helping Ben back to the keeper's house. "Sorry—I lost him. Let's get you inside and have a look. You're bleeding."

Monty half-dragged Ben into the kitchen. "Sit tight and try not to fall out of your chair." Monty let Ben slip through his grasp into a seat at the table. "I'm going to get you ice and ibuprofen."

This certainly wasn't the first time Ben had been soundly clocked and probably wouldn't be the last. The chill in the air told him that Jon's ghost had manifested. When he lifted his head, he saw the spirit standing on the far side of the room, watching him with concern.

"Thank you," Ben said, hating the way his voice shook in the adrenaline crash of the fight's aftermath. "You saved my life."

Ben had the feeling that his assailant had wanted to deal a beat-down more than he was motivated by robbery. He felt pretty sure that he could rule out random homophobia, and the guy had never tried to snatch Ben's watch or demand money.

Was I followed and didn't pick up on it? There's no reason for anyone to jump me, except for that Erik and I are stirring the pot again, dredging up old secrets.

Monty returned with a glass of water and two tablets. "Here. Take these. And let me check you over. I might need to drive you to the E.R."

Ben accepted the pills and drink gratefully. He endured Monty's field triage, trying not to squeeze his eyes shut against the flashlight beam as the lighthouse keeper checked his pupils.

"I've had worse. I'm okay," Ben argued.

Monty sat back in his chair. "Maybe. You probably should go get it checked out."

Wouldn't be my first untreated concussion or bruised bone. Ben winced as he shifted in his seat. "Both of you saved my ass."

"Glad we could help. Jon and I were watching that baking show on the streaming network when all of a sudden he blinked out, and I knew something was wrong."

"Did you catch the guy?" Ben asked, reminding himself that he needed to go meet Sean.

Monty shook his head. "By the time I got there, he was gone. Jon's range is limited, and he chose to stay with you. Sorry."

Ben shook his head, then thought better of it as the pain grayed his vision. "That's fine. Just asking."

"Do you know who jumped you?"

This time, Ben resisted the urge to shake his head. "He seemed familiar, but I can't place him. He didn't try to rob me, so he must have followed me here. And since I was watching for a tail, that means he's not an amateur."

"Were you just out for a walk, or did you need something?" Monty plugged in his electric kettle and soon had steaming hot cups of tea in front of both of them at the table. Now that the danger was over, Jon's ghost was no longer visible. Ben wondered whether Monty had helped the spirit take a more solid shape or if it was something Jon could do for a limited time. Jon had manifested looking more lifelike than any of the other ghosts Ben had glimpsed.

"I'm still trying to solve Cafaro's murder," Ben said. "I can't explain why, except that I think it's important to wrap up that period in the town's history and heal some wounds. And I wondered if Jon had thought of anything since we talked. You never know when something small turns out to be the missing piece."

Monty stared off into space, and Ben figured he and Jon were having a conversation. "Jon wants you to tell him again what happened after he died. Obviously, that's not something he remembers, but he's willing to see if something strikes him as odd."

"Okay—here we go," Ben said, ignoring the headache. "Voorhis and his *strega* argued, Voorhis killed him, and the witch cursed Voorhis as he died. Then Cafaro killed Voorhis—and Peter Duncan, the producer, got a photo of Cafaro with the gun and the body. He hid it in an old clock along with incriminating ledgers and hid the clock in the window seat of the B&B where he was staying."

He paused to sip his tea. "Cafaro must have realized that Duncan had become a threat, because he had him killed too," Ben recapped. "Which left a lot of unhappy people—the remaining cast and crew who were out of jobs, the businesses and their employees that depended on having movie money spent here, the city boosters who wanted the publicity and the celebrities, and anyone who invested in the films or the Regent Theater."

"That's a lot of people with motive," Monty said.

"Yeah," Ben agreed. "Then Cafaro got blown sky-high by a car bomb. It didn't bring back the theater or the movie business, and it spelled the beginning of the end for the Commodore Wilson Hotel. For all we know, his murder might not have even been related to the movies—Cafaro was in deep with the Newark Mob and might have double-crossed someone who had nothing to do with Cape May."

"And you said that Erik saw Cafaro's ghost?' Monty asked, intrigued.

"He doesn't have the same kind of ability you have—Erik can't channel spirits. But he can see them sometimes—so can I. He got the sense that Cafaro expected resolution. Nobody benefits from having his ghost hanging around. It might be a good idea to solve his murder and let him move on."

Ben wasn't sure why a mobster like Cafaro would want to hurry to the afterlife given what was probably waiting for him, but maybe it was better than limbo.

Once again, Monty had that glazed expression that signaled a silent conversation with his ghost partner. "Jon wants to know more about the car bomb," Monty said finally.

The ibuprofen was kicking in, and Ben's head didn't hurt as much, making it easier to think. "Cafaro was in New York City, and his car exploded. Killed him and his driver. From the accounts, it was a pretty spectacular blast."

Monty's head came up quickly and he winced. "Quit yelling," he snapped, and it took Ben a moment to realize that Monty was talking to Jon.

"Jon says that the bomb is the clue. Robert Bowers, the director, was left with nothing. Everything he'd worked for fell apart because Cafaro was a self-destructive, vengeful asshole. Bowers was ex-military—from an explosives unit. He'd call in old army buddies to set the explosions in the movies."

Ben remembered Jon saying that before, but at the time he'd been more focused on other parts of the ghost's story. "Would any of those people commit murder for Bowers?"

Monty listened again, then nodded. "Jon says that Bowers told all kinds of war stories. He was tight with his buddies and said they'd been to hell and back together. One of the explosives guys told Jon that Bowers was their commander and that he was the only reason they made it back alive. So, yeah. Not too much of a stretch that they might rig a car for him. Everyone knew Cafaro was scum."

"That was more than sixty years ago," Ben mused. "No telling whether Bowers or the bomber is even still alive. They'd have to be around ninety years old. We have a solid theory—but no proof. And if he's gotten away with murder this long, I doubt Bowers is going to confess or turn himself in."

"Does it matter?" Monty asked. "Even if you could prove it, they don't usually send guys that old up the river. Hell, given how many people's lives Cafaro ruined, folks would probably want to give Bowers a medal."

Since Cafaro had ordered the killing of Jon's lover and black-mailed Jon into the situation that cost him his life, Ben figured the ghost probably thought Cafaro got what was coming to him.

"As an ex-cop, I can't really approve," Ben said. He thought about the night he had feared he would lose Erik to someone willing to kill to keep the past buried. *If things had gone differently, if Erik had died...I might have been willing to pull the trigger on his killer myself.*

He cleared his throat. "But if I'd been in Jon's shoes, I can see where my opinion would be different."

"What now?" Monty asked.

Ben shrugged. "I'll look Bowers up and see what happened to him. Not sure there's more to be done than that. Erik and Alessia are working on the *strega* curse." His phone vibrated, and a glance told him Sean was at the garage. "And I've got another situation to deal with. As for Cafaro's ghost...maybe he'll get dragged to hell where he belongs."

Ben's headache had eased, although he suspected he'd have a colorful bruise on the side of his face tomorrow.

Monty insisted on coming out onto his porch to make sure Ben's attacker hadn't returned and waved as Ben drove away. Ben forced down his worry for Erik. He had a cousin to save.

NINE

BEN

"That's a good-looking truck," Ben said after Sean pulled into the oversized garage. "I hope you give yourself credit. You said you were going to get your own food truck, and you did it. I'm proud as hell of you—and I know Aunt Meg and Uncle Stewart are too."

"Thanks," Sean said. "That means the world to me. Or it will, when we're not hiding from the Mob."

"It's dark enough that I don't think anyone noticed you pulling in here," Ben said. "That's why I kept the outside light off. Plus, there's not much traffic on this street. Help me pull those tarps over it, just in case." He and Sean unfolded the big sheets, and Ben stepped up onto the running board to pull the tarp up over the front of the truck.

"What's all this with the speakers and lights?" Ben asked, getting a better look at the top of the vehicle.

Despite everything, Sean grinned a wide, toothy smile that reminded Ben of when they were kids. "It's got a sound system like you wouldn't believe. The subwoofer rocks the whole truck. And the lights have a dozen different patterns and even more colors. When I crank them both up, it's like Close Encounters!"

Some things never changed. Ben remembered watching that old movie over and over when Sean was in his UFO phase. "Congratulations—you've finally got your very own spaceship. If you decide to take off for Devil's Tower, just remember—pictures or it didn't happen."

"You've got it," Sean replied, even as his grin faded. "Might not be a bad idea if the fuckin' *Mob* is after me."

"Hitching a ride to another planet with aliens you don't know is never a good option," Ben said, straight-faced, relieved they were falling back into the banter that had helped him survive his teen years.

"I guess." As quickly as the good mood had come, it dissipated, leaving Sean looking scared and uncertain.

"Hey. We'll figure it out. Just hang in there for me, okay?"

Sean swallowed hard and nodded as they finished covering up the truck. He kept lookout while Ben locked up, and once they climbed into Ben's car, Sean slumped in his seat. "So...which rental unit can I squat in?"

"Your mom and dad own all of them, so it's really not 'squatting,'" Ben reminded him. "They're more yours than mine, by a long shot."

"You wanted the family business. I didn't. Yada, yada." Sean closed his eyes. "We're coming into the off-season. Vacancies shouldn't be hard to come by."

Ben cleared his throat. "Erik invited you to stay at his place. I'll be there as well. We mostly live together—well, not exactly, but pretty much except for changing mailing addresses."

"Congrats," Sean replied, eyes still closed. "And you really want me crashing your love nest?"

Ben leaned his head back dramatically. "Don't ever call it that again." Sean's wicked laugh told Ben the comment had the desired effect.

"Just for that, we won't be quiet," Ben threatened, waggling his eyebrows to assure that Sean knew exactly what he meant.

"Dude—I live with three guys. You think they never have overnight company? Earplugs are a necessity, so I don't have to bleach my brain."

"Speaking of your friends—when things calm down, Erik wants Mateo to ink him."

That got Sean to open his eyes. "Seriously? I didn't think Erik was the tattoo type."

Ben felt slightly offended on Erik's behalf. "Meaning what?"

"Don't get your panties in a twist. I'm not throwing shade on your boo."

"Oh, God. Please don't use that word."

"Bae?"

"Just shoot me now."

"Seriously, what? Boyfriend? Significant other? Partner? *Fi-an-cé?*" He dragged out the syllables like a teasing taunt on that last word.

Ben must have twitched because Sean cackled in triumph. "Oh, my God. I don't see a ring, but you're thinking about it?"

"Shut up."

"Tell me."

"Sean—"

"It would take my mind off my troubles," Sean said with an exaggerated pleading look that reminded Ben of the schlocky paintings of sad-eyed children he'd seen when he was a kid.

"Alright, already," Ben said in surrender. "Yes. Maybe. Just—not yet. But maybe. Erik's the one. I know it. He's way out of my league, but for some crazy reason, he loves me. And we're good together, Sean. Like—*really* good." Ben probably sounded as uncomfortable as he felt, voicing his feelings. But he and Sean had always been honest with each other, and Ben didn't want to lose that.

"Ben and Erik, sitting in a tree...K-I-S-S—"

"What are you, ten?"

"Growing up is optional, bro. I'm hanging onto the glory days." Sean shot him a grin, and Ben thought they might actually be okay.

"Before zits and shaving?"

Sean nodded. "And taxes, and adulting—"

"You have a point."

"Seriously—I'm happy for you. You deserve it. And I guess that means you're staying in Cape May?"

Ben nodded. "You are officially off the hook for running the business. Unless you changed your mind?" As hesitant as Ben had been early on, the thought of not continuing with the rental company made him unexpectedly sad.

"Don't sweat it—I'm not cut out for the family business," Sean assured him. "Mom says you're doing an awesome job. It suits you."

Ben huffed out a breath. "Except that I've used my PI license more in the past few months than I expected, trying to keep the past from catching up with Erik and me."

"You guys ever think about going into WITSEC?" Sean's tone was joking, but his eyes were serious.

Ben shrugged. "I'm small potatoes. Erik—maybe. Looking into the case we're working, I realized he was a big fish in his world before he came here. And if he wanted to go into protection, I'd go with him. But…that's not on the table."

Much as he loved and trusted Sean, he couldn't tell him about the supernatural side of Erik's shop or the witches and spells that had somehow become "normal" for Ben in just a few months. *And I certainly can't mention the vampire business partner who takes cursed objects off his hands and saved his life in Antwerp.*

"I'm sorry about bringing trouble to your doorstep."

Ben reached over and gripped Sean's shoulder, giving him a fond shake. "You came home. That's how it's supposed to work."

Sean sighed, and Ben took it as agreement.

"Did I tell you that the Arts Council is going to renovate the Regent Theater and open it back up again?" Ben asked.

"That's great. I heard so many stories about that place in its glory days." Sean sat up straighter in his seat. "I always wanted to see it the way it used to be. If they can recreate that, it would be amazing."

"The theater's history is tangled up with the Mob—are you surprised?"

"No. Because of course it is. This is New Jersey," Sean replied.

"Newark Mob—not Russian."

"Because that's better?" Sean raised an eyebrow.

"Not really."

"I thought the Regent was long gone. Didn't they build a convenience store where it used to be?"

Ben shook his head. "They just boarded up the theater part and turned the old lobby into the store. Believe it or not, the Regent has been there the whole time."

Ben took the long way home, checking to make sure no one was following them. The sidewalks were mostly empty, now that the town belonged to the locals again. Ben slowed as they approached the boarded-up remains of the store.

"It doesn't look like much," Ben said. "The marquee is long gone, and they'll have to completely rebuild the front lobby that got turned into the shop, but the theater itself is better preserved than you'd think, according to Erik—"

"What's that guy doing?"

Ben looked where Sean pointed to see a man prying one of the sheets of plywood loose. At his feet was a gas can. As the stranger pulled the wood back, a white light flared from inside the abandoned store, tossing him onto his ass a few feet away.

"Shit." Ben swerved to park at the curb. Without a word, he and Sean were out of the car in an instant and running. Ben resolutely ignored the way his pounding steps made his head throb. He'd worked through pain before on busts, and he could do it again.

The man saw them coming and ran, leaving his gas can behind. Sean pulled ahead and launched into a flying tackle. Both he and the stranger hit the sidewalk with a bone-jarring thud. The would-be arsonist struggled, but he couldn't throw Sean off. Ben hid a snicker, figuring that Sean's love for rugby finally paid off.

Ben had his phone in hand before he caught up to where Sean had the man pinned. "Nine-one-one? I want to report an attempted arson at the old Regent Theater. We caught the guy, so can you please send a car to pick him up?"

So much for keeping Sean's presence in Cape May low key. Ben still couldn't make out the vandal's features in the dim light, but he frowned when he saw familiar stripes on the sleeve of his jacket.

"Fuck. He's the one who jumped me at the lighthouse." Ben used the light on his phone to get a better look at the man's face and to take a picture. "Enzo Rossi." He dredged the name up from his memory, a reminder of his undercover days.

"Don't know what you're talking about, pal," Rossi taunted.

Sean shifted his weight, resetting his stocky frame so that his knee landed on Rossi's hand.

"What the hell? Get off me!"

Sean let his knee take more of his weight while most of his body kept the assailant's torso immobile. "Broken fingers are a real bitch," Sean said. Ben knew every one of Sean's fingers were just a bit crooked, a souvenir from rugby. "But it's harder to set the hand and wrist. So—why did you jump him at the lighthouse?"

"Okay!" Rossi cursed loudly, then went limp in Sean's hold. Sean kept his full weight from descending onto the hand beneath his knee.

Faintly, Ben heard sirens. He hoped Rossi talked fast.

"It was dumb luck—I saw him get into his car, and I recognized him as the lying undercover bastard that fucked us all over," the man spat. "It wasn't why I came here, but I didn't mind getting extra paybacks since I was already in town."

"And the theater? Why were you going to set the fire?"

"Screw you."

Sean shifted again, and the man cried out. "Alright! Fuck. Some folks back home didn't want to see the theater renovated. Said it needed to stay dead and buried like the guy who used to own it."

"Voorhis?"

"Who?"

Ben raised an eyebrow. "Cafaro?"

"Yeah. That's the name."

Ben knew mobsters held grudges, but Cafaro must have been a real son of a bitch for the hate to be this strong sixty-plus years after his death. "By 'back home,' you mean Newark?"

He could hear sirens coming closer. Once the cops got here, he'd lose his chance to ask questions. Sean didn't have to move much to get the answer.

"Yes! Newark. Now get this moose off my fucking hand."

Two patrol cars screeched to a stop, lights flashing, doors slamming open. "Police! Stay where you are! Put your hands where we can see them and don't move."

Ben sighed. Getting arrested wasn't on his to-do list for the evening, but he imagined that saving the Regent—and its whole block —from going up in flames was worth it.

"I'm the one who called you. We saw him trying to break in. His gas can is by the doorway," Ben said as the cop cuffed him. "Chased him and caught him for you."

"Next time, leave that to us," the cop replied, tugging Ben to his feet. Ben's head swam for a second.

"I want to press charges," Ben said. "He attacked me earlier tonight at the lighthouse. I have witnesses."

A second cop cuffed Sean and pulled him away so a third officer could restrain Rossi. The fourth cop was back with the gas can.

"You can tell your story to the chief," Ben's cop said as he pushed Ben into the back seat of his cruiser, as Sean got in from the other side.

"That's what I was hoping," Ben muttered. He had no illusions about Chief Hendricks being happy to see him.

"Much as it pains me to admit it, you were right about the perp having ties to the Bianchi family." Hendricks sat at the table in the interrogation room where Ben and Sean had spent the last half hour waiting in silence.

Ben opened his mouth to say "told you so," and Hendricks glared. "Don't." Ben sat back, and Sean snickered.

"Want to walk me through what you think is going on? Because you always have the best stories to tell," Hendricks said, pissed off but willing to listen.

Ben couldn't really fault the police chief. With Hendricks, it was more butting antlers than measuring dicks, more about defending territory than exerting dominance. Hendricks wanted Ben to remember that he wasn't a cop anymore, and Ben wanted Hendricks to respect his experience and instincts. Being close to the same age just added fuel.

"Here's the 'too long, didn't read' summary," Ben said. "The guy we collared recognized me from the bust that nearly killed me and wanted personal payback. I couldn't place him at first because he changed his look, but then it clicked. Name is Enzo Rossi, loyal as fuck to his boss and mean as a snake. He got sent to burn down the Regent because someone in Newark still hates Vincente Cafaro. Meanwhile, the Russian Mob is shaking down food truck owners in Wildwood for protection money—which is why Sean is hiding out here."

Hendricks's gaze flickered to Sean. "Great job on the hiding part. Real stealthy."

"And a priceless figurine that disappeared in a heist run by the Russian Mob several years ago got sent to the Arts Council—we think it's because the sender wanted to set the Russians after Erik."

"Fuck, Nolan! Why is this the first I'm hearing about that?"

Ben fixed Hendricks with a level gaze. "Because the Feds told Erik to keep it between him and them. I'm telling you because the guy who sent it—Joakim Denikin—is in deep with the Russians. I thought maybe you could arrest him, at the very least, for receiving stolen property before he gets Erik killed. Maybe tack on some charges about using the US Mail—"

Hendricks rubbed his temples. Ben wondered if the chief's headache was as bad as his own. "Assault, attempted arson, two warring Mob factions, extortion, and grand theft—is this your idea of 'just another Saturday night'?"

Ben knew Hendricks believed him. He had a shiner and blood from a cut to his scalp to prove the assault charge, as well as Monty's testimony. The gas can sealed the deal, probably covered with the perp's prints. Erik might be upset that Ben had let slip about the figurine, but between the food truck problem and the statuette, a bookie would probably put good odds on the Russians making an appearance to cause trouble.

And I left out the part about the ghosts, the spooky flash of light at the theater, and the fact that Erik and Alessia are trying to break the strega's *curse to save Jaxon. Geez—I took it easy on the guy.*

"And Rossi just happened to spill his guts to you?" Hendricks pinned Ben and Sean with a glare. Ben glared back, and Sean managed the harmless choirboy look that had gotten him out of all kinds of scrapes when he was younger.

"Some guys piss themselves when they get scared—others get chatty," Ben said, daring Hendricks to blink first. "We got lucky."

"Shit. You know, the damnedest thing is I believe you. We ran the prints and came up with Rossi's name. Don't know anything about Denikin or a missing figurine, but we've heard rumors about the protection racket in Wildwood. I was hoping it wouldn't affect Cape May, but—oh, well." He shook his head. "I should bust both of you for unauthorized restraint, but if Rossi had set that fire, it could have taken out half the downtown."

Hendricks took a deep breath and closed his eyes, but if he was seeking peace, Ben doubted the chief would find it tonight.

"Show me the evidence you've got to warrant a visit to the guy you think sent the stolen figurine," Hendricks said, conceding defeat.

"Give me my phone back, and I'll email it," Ben countered.

Hendricks went to the door, said something to the officer outside, and returned with both men's phones after a few moments. Ben made sure to shield his log-in from the security camera, and in a few keystrokes, sent the files on Denikin to the address Hendricks supplied.

"I'll go have a look on my computer," Hendricks said. "Be right back. Don't go anywhere," he added with a smirk.

He left Ben and Sean alone again. They sat in silence, knowing they were being recorded. Hendricks returned faster than Ben expected, and the annoyance on the man's face had shifted to worry.

"Doesn't look like Denikin is an upstanding addition to the neighborhood," he observed in a wry tone. "Both he and Rossi have ghosted on their parole officers...which is cause enough to put them in custody." He sighed. "It's still reasonably early. Might as well grab Denikin before he skips town. We'll pick him up tonight."

"Thank you for believing me," Ben said.

Hendricks gave him an annoyed look. "I'm not doing this for you, Nolan. My mother thinks the world of your partner. I'd never hear the end of it if he got hurt on my watch."

Susan Hendricks was a force of nature. Ben was glad to have her on their side.

"Are we free to go?" Ben asked.

Hendricks glared at him, then nodded. "Yeah. Just try to stay out of trouble for the rest of the night. We're going to be busy."

Ben hid a smile. "We'll do our best. Come on, Sean. We need to get you settled."

On the steps to the police station, a dark-haired woman in a pantsuit blocked their way and shoved a microphone at Ben and Erik. "What was it like, stopping the Regent Theater arsonist?"

Ben tried to sidestep, but she matched his move as if they were dancing. "Come on—you're heroes! Make a statement. You saved downtown Cape May. You deserve a little fame."

He glanced at the press pass that hung on a lanyard around the woman's neck. *Emma Hanson, WIGN-TV,* and realized why she looked vaguely familiar.

"No comment." Ben grabbed Sean's elbow to steer him around the reporter, signaling with his tight grip for Sean to remain silent. To Ben's chagrin, he saw Hanson's cameraman standing on the sidewalk, meaning that his face and Sean's would be all over the evening news. His heart sank, realizing that stopping the arson meant putting Sean in more danger.

"Is it true that rival Mob families are fighting over who controls Cape May?" Hanson pressed, following them down the steps. "Ben Nolan—you took on the Mob in Newark. Are you here in Cape May to bust mobsters?"

Ben's gut clenched and he felt his temper rise. Dealing with media had always been one of the worst parts of high-profile busts. *I'd almost take a bullet over being interviewed. At least with the bullet, I get painkillers to put me out of my misery.*

"No comment," he said through gritted teeth.

"If you change your mind, call me." Hanson pressed her card into Sean's hand, and Sean pocketed it on reflex.

Ben guided Sean away from the small crowd that had formed in front of the police station toward where he had left his car. Once they were inside with the doors locked, Ben let out his breath in a relieved *woosh.*

"Sorry about that," he said as they burned rubber pulling away from the curb. "Hendricks was right—this is a lousy way to hide you."

Sean shrugged. "It is what it is. I couldn't live with myself if you'd let that guy break in and burn down the theater on my account." He shot Ben a grin. "Be like Elsa—let it go."

"If you break into song, so help me, I will shove you out of a moving car and leave your ass in the middle of the street."

"Yeah, yeah, yeah. I'm scared." Sean managed a wan grin after all they'd been through.

"I'm all for reporters—except when they're after me," Ben confessed. "I'm sure I'll say something stupid on camera and make everything worse. And maybe I'm wrong. Maybe letting her shine a spotlight on what's going on would make the cockroaches scatter. I reacted back there—I didn't think."

"It's been a long day," Sean replied. "Cut yourself a break. We're alive. Everything else can be fixed."

They took a roundabout route to throw off anyone who might try to follow them and headed to Erik's house. The shop on the first floor was dark except for the security lights. Ben could tell from a glance upstairs that Erik must still be with Alessia since only the timed light was on. His instincts were on high alert, and Sean seemed edgy as well, watching their surroundings as Ben used his key on the door to the apartment's entrance and disarmed the security system.

"Upstairs," he said, switching on the light. As soon as they were inside, he locked the door and activated the alarm. Sean didn't need to know about the wardings, but they made Ben feel safer.

"We used to ride past this shop on our bikes when we were kids," Sean said as they climbed the steep wooden steps. "Back when that old guy ran it."

"I remember," Ben replied. "We joked about it being haunted."

"Is it?"

Sean's question took Ben by surprise. "You believe in ghosts?"

Sean gave him a look. "I can't see them. But you could."

Ben had forgotten, but now the memories came back clearly. Aunt Meg had put the two of them to work cleaning units between tenants, which meant they were in and out of all the properties. Enough of the rentals were remodeled old homes that ghosts came with the territory. After all, this was Cape May, known for peaceful and mostly friendly haunts.

There had been plenty of times when odd occurrences got chalked up to ghostly activity while they were cleaning. Doors and drawers would open and close on their own, small items disappeared only to be found in improbable places, and sudden cold spots defied explanation. Ben had glimpsed a few ghosts, but none of the spirits ever bothered them.

"Trinkets isn't haunted, and neither is the apartment. There are, uh, actually *protections* in place to keep us extra safe."

He led Sean into the apartment and found himself strangely nervous about what his cousin would think even though the space belonged to Erik.

"Nice. Homey. And more modern than I pictured," Sean said. "Guess I expected 'creepy Victorian.' Not that I would have complained. I appreciate Erik inviting me to stay. I'd sleep in the truck if I needed to."

He set down his backpack and small duffel. "What did you mean by 'protections'?"

Ben cursed himself for his slip of the tongue, then remembered that this was Sean, who had grown up in Cape May. Maybe telling the whole truth wouldn't seem all that strange to Sean.

"Magic is real. So are curses. Sometimes the objects that come to Trinkets are haunted or dangerous. Erik can sense that, and he takes care of the ones that could hurt someone."

"Huh. What else?" Sean perched on the arm of the couch, taking Ben's revelation in stride.

"There are a lot of people in town with 'extra' talents. Some of them work together to try to keep the town safe. The Regent Theater has a curse on it. A friend is in the hospital right now because of that. Erik's working with a witch to try to break the spell."

Sean gave Ben a considered look. "I'd always heard stories, but I didn't know how much was hype for the tourists. If Mom and Dad knew for sure, they never said anything. I don't know whether you were expecting me to run away screaming, but I always hoped the rumors were true, so you kinda made my day. It makes the world more interesting."

"So magic is a 'secret' that everyone knows and no one talks about? How did I spend all those summers here and no one told me?" Ben asked, aggrieved.

Sean shrugged and followed Ben to the kitchen as Ben got them both beer from the fridge. "Dunno. You were gone for most of the year, and it never really came up. Plus, it was 'grown-up' stuff, and we were kids."

"Well, we're grown-ups now," Ben said, raising his bottle in a toast, clinking against Sean's.

"Adulting sucks. Just saying."

Ben didn't feel like cooking, so he and Sean made sandwiches, grabbed a big bag of chips and a couple of cold beers, and sat at the kitchen table.

"Do we know how to live it up, or what?" Ben asked, feeling the day's events in his bruised cheek, swollen eye, and the utter exhaustion now that the adrenaline rush had faded.

Sean raised his bottle in salute. "Just like the old days. Deadpool and Spider-Man!"

Ben chuckled, remembering. They had both liked Batman, but neither one wanted to be Robin. They teamed up as the "other" dynamic duo for their pre-teen adventures, much to Aunt Meg's amusement. Ben's large Spider-Man statue was his tribute to those days, and he suspected that Sean's framed Deadpool posters were the same for him.

"Sitting on Rossi was a stroke of genius." Ben grinned. "I will never diss rugby again."

"Better not," Sean mock-warned. "I went to the championships and kept both ears."

Ben shook his head, not wanting to think about the stories of rugby-gone-wrong that led to missing body parts. "D'ya mind? We're eating."

Sean snorted. "Seriously? When did you get a tender stomach? Or did you forget those gross-out jokes you loved to tell?"

"I don't have a tender stomach," Ben responded with feigned outrage. "I just gained more refined tastes."

"Keep telling yourself that."

Ben reached for a chip just as a loud crash sounded on the street in front of the house, and his car alarm wailed.

"What the fuck?" He ran to the window and looked down. A Toyota sedan had rammed into the side of his car, and the driver lay slumped over the steering wheel behind a badly-cracked windshield. Ben used his remote to silence the alarm.

"Call nine-one-one!" Ben ordered. He stuck his phone in his pocket and slid his Glock 19 into the back of his belt before heading to the door. "The driver's hurt."

He left Sean in the apartment and hurried down the steps. Police training had covered advanced first aid, intended to keep an injured person alive until EMTs could arrive. Ben wondered how big Hendricks's department was and whether anyone was left to respond, since he'd handed off Rossi and also tied up a couple of officers retrieving Denikin.

That's what the Fire Department is for, he thought as he hurried out the front door.

Ben winced when he saw the damage to his car, with the driver's side pushed in and the windows smashed. But his attention shifted quickly to the Toyota, worried about the driver...who was missing.

He felt the muzzle of a gun jab into his back. "Keep walking and don't look back," a voice said behind him. Ben felt someone remove his gun from his waistband.

Right on cue, a black SUV pulled up, and the rear door opened.

"Get in." The muzzle poked him in the ribs for emphasis.

Ben weighed his odds of survival between putting up a fight here on a public street where Sean might be watching from the window, and Susan might notice from next door. The gun shifted to his spine as if his kidnapper guessed his thoughts.

"Don't."

He'd be dead or paralyzed before he hit the ground. The gunman couldn't miss. Ben let himself be herded into the back of the SUV. The gun pressed against his head now, convincing him not to fight as his wrists were zip-tied together.

"Who are you?" Ben figured they owed him that much.

"We came after your cousin to make an example of him," the gunman said as the driver pulled away, just as sirens screamed in the distance. "Then we found out a much bigger fish could be caught... with you as bait."

Ben couldn't pick up any trace of an accent in the voice, but his answer made it clear that he was working for the Russians. *Shit. They're going to use me to get to Erik.*

"Your cousin needed to be taught a lesson," the driver chimed in. "But the price on Mitchell's head was too good to pass up."

Ben felt sick. *Erik has a Mob bounty on him? Maybe WITSEC would have been a good idea after all. It's not too late—Erik could still be protected.*

He could breathe again when the gun moved away from his head, but it now pressed against his side, making a point-blank stomach wound inevitable if he struggled. These guys were pros, and Ben wasn't likely to get an easy break.

"Erik retired. He's not a threat to you now."

The driver laughed, a cold sound that sent an icy slither down Ben's back. "Like he couldn't get called in to consult whenever they need him."

"He wouldn't go."

Dark, soulless eyes met his in the rearview mirror. "He wouldn't have a choice. The people he worked for don't ask—they demand.

Mitchell caused a lot of problems and cost people a lot of money. If someone takes him out—problem solved."

The sirens faded in the distance, and Ben realized that even if Sean had reported his capture to the 911 operator, the delay in conveying that information to the squad cars let his kidnappers make their escape. As for Susan, the SUV was unremarkable, and she'd never be able to read the plates.

I've got to get away or force their hand before they demand that Erik makes a trade. Because he will. I can't let him.

Ben hadn't given up. That stubbornness got him out of a lot of dicey situations. Sooner or later, his captors would make a mistake. If he saw a chance, he resolved to take it, however slim the odds. But if it came down to letting Erik save him by trading his own life, Ben balked.

I want to survive. I want to settle down with Erik and get old. But I won't let him die for me. I'll force their hand. After all, there's not much leverage in a dead hostage.

Making that decision let a strange calm settle over Ben. He had Plan A—escape, and Plan B—keep Erik safe. He doubted that he could make good on Plan C—take some of these sons of bitches down with him, but he resolved to do his best to make that happen.

Any distraction I provide might save lives if the cops try to make a raid. These guys can't shoot with their full attention if they've got to worry about me.

Ben resolved to watch and wait.

TEN

ERIK

"I know that after the last assignment, you needed some time off," Tim said. "But you made a difference. Bring the figurine up to DC. We'll sit down and talk. We can find a way you can contribute and still carve out time for yourself."

Erik took a few deep breaths, trying to rein in his temper. "You're missing the point. I'm out. I'm going to stay out. I did my part and paid a price for it. *Done.*" He paused. "We know who sent the statuette. No thanks to you."

"There's a lot going on."

"I'm sure there is, for you. My focus is a little more...narrow."

"Erik—"

"No. Figuring that out should have been done by your people, not my partner," Erik said, too keyed up for diplomacy. "You dropped the ball. If you want the figurine, come to Cape May and pick it up. Oh, and by the way, just be prepared—somehow we've become the dueling ground between the Russians and the Newark Mob. Because apparently the Feds haven't done their fucking job."

Tim was silent for a moment. Erik wondered when things changed. Before, he never doubted that Tim had his back. Now, Erik had to face the very real possibility that he'd only ever been a valuable asset to be coddled and manipulated. Or that the game had changed, and he and Ben had become pawns.

"Okay. You're right—you've done more than your share. I'll send my guys to pick up the figurine. Thank you. What you did matters."

Erik thought Tim was really saying goodbye. He didn't want to examine the tangle of emotions in his gut right now. "You're welcome."

He ended the call and stared at the phone in his hand.

"Are you alright?" Alessia asked.

Erik shook himself out of his trance. "Yeah. Just—one of my old bosses."

Alessia gave him a knowing glance as if she could read his mind. *Hell, maybe she can.*

Alessia's laptop buzzed with a reminder to start the video call with Travis Dominick and Teag Logan. Travis joined first. The ex-priest was a couple of years younger than Erik, with chin-length, crow-black hair, pale skin, and green eyes. Teag was next, good looking and slender, late twenties, with a skater boy mop of dark hair. A third person popped up on the call, someone Erik didn't recognize.

"Hey, I brought a friend—hope that's okay," Teag said. "This is Archibald Donnelly, and he's a necromancer."

"At your service," Donnelly said. He was a florid-faced man who looked to be in his late sixties, with Victorian-style muttonchop sideburns.

"We can use all the help we can get," Alessia replied. "Thank you for being on the call."

"We found out something that might be the glue that pulls it all together," Erik said. "Anna and I were going through another couple of boxes of donated memorabilia. I knew as soon as I walked in that something with wicked-powerful resonance was in the box. Not magical or dangerous," he clarified. "But stained by extremely strong emotions."

"What was it?" Travis asked. Erik guessed that the ex-priest's mediumship and psychic visions gave him a unique perspective, as did his experience as a demon hunter.

"An engraved locket," Erik replied. "There was a note attached, explaining that the sender used to work at the convenience store and would sneak off to explore the old theater. He found it in what seemed to be a private apartment on the second floor and thought it might have belonged to someone famous. As soon as I touched it, I knew."

"Don't keep us in suspense!" Teag said.

"I got whammied," Erik admitted. "Laid out flat on my back by the strength of the resonance. Here's the short version, based on what I saw in my vision plus a little creative interpretation. Thomas Ruccio, the *strega*, was in love with Benjamin Voorhis, the theater owner. He agreed to help him make the theater a success, and they became lovers. But it was the Fifties, and while Ruccio was something of a hermit, Voorhis felt the need to be seen with an ever-changing parade of starlets."

Erik grimaced. "I got the feeling that Voorhis's affairs weren't just window dressing. I'm betting that Voorhis slept with the starlets and flaunted the relationships. Meanwhile, he led Ruccio on, pretending to care and using their relationship to manipulate the *strega*. Then Voorhis began to fear Ruccio and took advantage of the witch's trust. He shot Ruccio during an argument."

"Because that couldn't possibly go wrong," Travis muttered.

Erik nodded. "Yeah. Ruccio cursed Voorhis with his dying breath."

"We think he overshot the mark," Alessia took up the story. "It was an improvised curse, sloppy and vengeful. He didn't just curse Voorhis. He cursed the theater itself and by extension everyone who 'owned' it. Which included Vincente Cafaro and the people who bought the property down through the years to Jaxon."

"That's some story," Teag said. "Is the body in the theater?"

Erik shook his head. "We thought that until I got the vision from the locket. It must have been something Ruccio carried on him—probably a gift from Voorhis—that fell off when he was killed. Voorhis took the body, muttered something about the landfill."

"Shit," Travis muttered.

"Yeah. I'm kinda siding with the *strega* on killing the asshole," Erik admitted. "I'm guessing the locket's chain broke, and it ended up under something—"

"Anchoring his spirit for close to seventy years," Donnelly completed the thought.

Erik nodded. "Yeah. There's no way we can find a body to burn or bury it."

"What about the locket?" Donnelly pressed. "If it was an emotionally important gift, it might symbolize the betrayal to the *strega*. Destroy it as part of the banishment ritual, and you can sever the spirit's connection. It's your best shot, without a corpse."

Erik and Alessia exchanged a look. "We can do that," Alessia said.

"Is there a way to destroy it that's better than others?" Erik asked. "Because we're only likely to get one shot at this. Either we banish him and break his hold on Jaxon and the theater—or Ruccio's ghost kills all three of us."

Erik couldn't help feeling sympathy for the *strega*. He had experienced the pain of a lover's betrayal before the move to Cape May. If he'd had the *strega's* magic at the moment when he discovered Josh's infidelity, Erik didn't want to think about what he might have done.

"And the banishment ritual we created—it'll work?" Erik asked.

"In all likelihood," Donnelly replied.

Erik just stared at the man. "Can we do a little better than 'maybe'? Because if we're wrong, Alessia and I are going to die."

"It should work," Donnelly said. "Short of burning the place down. But magic is an art, not a science. It can be dangerous to forget that."

Erik took the warning to heart, but at this point they were out of alternatives. "Assuming we can break the spell, how long will it take for Jaxon to improve?"

"If the magic is what's causing his illness, it should turn around as soon as the curse is removed," Donnelly replied. Travis nodded in agreement.

"That's what our witch friend, Rowan, said as well," Teag added.

"Good," Erik muttered, more to himself than to the others. "That's very good."

After that, they discussed the details of the items needed for the banishment and the ritual itself. By the time the video call ended, Erik had a clear road map of what they needed to do.

Assuming they were right. If not—

"C'mon," Alessia said. "We need to kick *strega* ass and send that bad bitch straight to hell."

"Hell, yes!" Erik agreed, with a level of certainty he didn't completely feel.

Erik checked his messages. He had turned off his phone while he and Alessia were crafting the ritual. He'd kept his magic focused on the task at hand all day, but that didn't keep him from worrying about Ben. When he and Ben had talked earlier about Sean, Erik hadn't hesitated to invite Ben's cousin to stay with them. He hoped Ben interpreted his willingness as complete support for doing whatever was necessary to protect Sean.

Now Erik's insecurities made him second-guess himself. *Did I do enough? Should I have done more?*

He and Alessia had been working for hours. Morning slipped into afternoon, and Erik found himself antsy, ready to eliminate the *strega's* threat. Arjun texted updates on Jaxon's condition, but nothing had changed. They needed to break the curse. He paused to read a text.

Ben: *Sean and I will be at your apartment—call if you need anything. Be careful. Russian and Newark players in town. Don't go anywhere alone. Love you. Be safe.*

Erik swallowed hard as he texted back, acknowledging the warning, urging Ben to be careful, returning the endearment.

"Something wrong?" Alessia asked, concerned.

Erik turned off his phone and slipped it in his pocket, then shook his head. "No. We're good. Let's get this over with."

He drove, with Alessia riding shotgun and everything they would need for the banishing ritual in a duffel in the back seat. They parked in a lot behind the theater, and Erik assured himself that the street was empty before using Jaxon's key to enter.

"Something's different," Alessia said as he locked the door behind them. "Can you feel it? A recent blast of energy. Very recent."

Erik nodded and swept the beam of his heavy-duty flashlight

around the empty shell of the convenience store. "There," he said, pointing to where shattered glass from one of the boarded-up windows covered the floor. "That wasn't broken before."

"You think someone tried to get in?"

"Sure looks like it."

While Alessia put down a protective circle of salt and set up a warded workspace to keep them safe from the curse's power, Erik concentrated on his intuition, picking up on strong emotional resonance and lingering supernatural energies. The impressions were jumbled, a tumult of anger, bitterness, and protectiveness. After so many decades, he wondered if that was all that remained of the *strega* —less of a vengeful ghost and more like an automatic defense that persisted long after the need had passed.

I saw an old TV show about a weapon that outlived its makers and just floated in space, destroying everything in its path because there was no way to turn it off. I think that's what happened here—the strega *cast the curse in a hurry, and it's long outlived its goal of getting vengeance on his killer. It's not even protecting the theater anymore, or it wouldn't have hurt Jaxon.*

"You with me?" Alessia's voice jolted Erik from his thoughts.

"Yeah. Just seeing what I could pick up from the energy. I'm ready."

Alessia had already chalked symbols inside the salt ring and lit candles set at the quarters. A weighted length of cord that had been soaked in salt and colloidal silver formed a second circle inside the loose salt.

Erik felt a frisson of energy as power rose around them, both inside and outside the circle. Alessia's familiar magic wrapped them in safety. Outside the circle, the *strega's* power simmered with anger, feral and malicious. Erik laid a hand on Alessia's shoulder, lending his energy and magic.

"Thomas Ruccio. Show yourself!" Alessia commanded. "By all that is holy, by the saints and prophets, by the powers above and those below, we summon you."

The air shimmered and the room grew cold. Erik fought the instinct to rub his arms to warm himself, but his shivering stemmed as much from fear as it did the sudden chill. Gradually, the ghost took shape.

Thomas Ruccio stood in the ruins of an abandoned convenience store nearly seventy years after his murder. Handsome and proud, he carried himself with confidence, even after his ignoble death.

"You were wronged," Alessia said. "And your vengeance has been served to everyone who had a hand in your betrayal. As well as to others who had no part, whose blood is on your head."

Ruccio's fury hit Erik like a punch to the gut, and he folded over on himself. "Keep going," he gasped to Alessia, breathing through the pain. "Don't stop."

Images assaulted him. Of the Regent as it was in its heyday, of Ruccio besotted by a man who didn't return his love, of Voorhis, cold and cruel, mocking his dying lover for being stupid enough to trust.

"Voorhis deserved what he got. So did Cafaro. But so many others since then...they did nothing to you," Erik managed. "This place...you have to let go."

Sorrow. Loss. Regret. Loneliness. And most of all, fury. Ruccio's second-hand emotions whipsawed through Erik despite the protections, blunted to a manageable level by the wardings.

"He saw the theater as the public symbol of his relationship with Voorhis." Erik forced the words out. "When Voorhis betrayed him, Ruccio wanted to take away the thing his lover loved more than him."

Outside their circle, Ruccio's ghost raged, sending the trash that littered the floor flying and slamming debris into the shimmering curtain of energy raised by Alessia's warding.

"You must go now," Alessia told the ghost. "It's time. Leave—or we will send you on."

She held the locket over a silver bowl filled with dried leaves known for their protective and cleansing properties, along with other powders to dispel evil and banish spirits.

Ruccio howled a plaintive wail of pain and fury and tried to tear at the protective barrier with his hands. It held, forcing him back. Desperation made the spirit seem nearly solid.

Mine! The word sounded so loudly in Erik's mind that he nearly fell to his knees. He usually couldn't hear spirits, but then again, he hadn't tangled with a witch ghost before. Ruccio's voice ached with grief and betrayal. Erik's heart broke for the *strega*, who even now, after everything, couldn't bear to lose the locket from his faithless lover.

"Keep going!" Erik yelled to Alessia.

The energy in the air sparked around them, raising the hair on the back of Erik's arms. Alessia's voice never faltered, even when Ruccio sent salvos of blindingly bright light against the wardings.

The spell itself was a combination exorcism and banishment, followed by a cleansing that both the ex-priest and the necromancer agreed would work. Erik hoped that they knew their stuff, because Ruccio did not show any indication of going gently into the night.

Alessia tossed a lit match into the bowl, and flames jumped. As she dropped the locket into the chalice, Ruccio screamed. Fire consumed the ghost, burning from the edges to the core until nothing remained.

The abrupt silence seemed as odd as the sudden change in temperature as the spectral chill warmed back to normal. Erik stood and realized his hands were shaking. The old store outside the warded circle remained still.

"Is it done? Is he gone?" Erik asked.

Alessia finished the words of the incantation, then turned to each of the candles in the circle and gave thanks before she closed the wardings and the iridescent protective curtain around the workspace vanished.

"It's over." Alessia looked around the shabby remains of the store, then closed her eyes and held out one hand, a gesture Erik knew meant she was feeling for any remaining presence of the vengeful *strega*.

The ominous sense of being watched that Erik had felt when he explored the theater was gone. He felt a prickle that he had come to understand meant that less powerful ghosts were present, but they did not manifest, and he did not sense any malice from them.

"Still haunted," he said.

Alessia shrugged. "What theater isn't? Adds authenticity."

Erik chuckled. "Yeah, I guess so. Jaxon would probably like to keep a few around, as long as they stop trying to push him down the stairs."

"I think the ghosts are as relieved to have Ruccio gone as we are," Alessia said. "They feared him. He grew worse as time passed. I believe we did him a mercy, although he didn't want to go."

"Why would he stay?" The Regent's glory days were far behind it, and enough time had passed since Ruccio was alive that the names and faces of that era were nearly forgotten. "His love was betrayed, the theater is in ruins, and he got his vengeance many times over."

"The living aren't the only ones who have trouble letting go of the past," Alessia said, snuffing out the candles and gathering up the ritual items. "He knew what was here. None of us know what lies beyond."

"Not even Teag's friend, the necromancer?" Erik wasn't a religious man, but the thought of what happened after death sometimes weighed heavy on his mind.

"If he knows, he probably won't tell."

"That sucks."

They locked the store and headed for Erik's car. As soon as they were outside, Erik turned his phone back on and called Arjun, putting the call on speaker. "How is Jaxon? Is there any change?"

At first, all he heard was Arjun sobbing, and Erik feared the worst. "Arjun?"

"He woke up." Arjun drew a ragged breath. "Just a couple of minutes ago. His eyes opened, and…just like that, he was awake. Whatever you and Alessia did…bless you."

Erik felt tears start, overcome by Arjun's gratitude and Jaxon's turnaround. He saw the same relief in Alessia's eyes.

"We broke the curse and banished the ghost of the man who cast it, so no one else will die because of the spell," he told Arjun. "Give Jaxon our best, and we'll be around to see him soon."

Erik scanned down through his missed calls, noting several from an unfamiliar number all within the past half hour. He pressed the number, curious, although he figured it would probably be spam.

"Erik?" The man sounded breathless and frightened.

"Who is this?"

"Sean. Ben's cousin. He left me your number."

"He left it? Where did he go?" Erik felt his good mood crash into gut-deep fear.

"Someone plowed into Ben's parked car. He went down to help the driver while I called 911. Then there was a black SUV, and they took Ben. I told the cops, but by the time they got here, he was long gone."

Erik swallowed hard and exchanged a worried glance with Alessia. "Did the cops say anything?"

"The car that hit Ben's was stolen," Sean replied. "I tried to find out more, but they wouldn't tell me anything. The lady next door came out and said she'd seen the same thing that I had. She invited me home with her, but I went back to your apartment. This is all my fault for drawing the Russians here. Erik—we've got to rescue Ben."

Erik struggled to hold it together. "The neighbor is Susan Hendricks—her son is the chief of police. She'll make sure this gets priority. You can trust her. Stay in the apartment. I'm heading there now. And it's not your fault—I was a fool to think I could forget the past."

"What are we going to do?"

"Sit tight for now. I'm on my way."

"Okay." Sean sounded jittery. "Whatever the plan is, I'm in."

"We'll talk when I get there. Don't go anywhere."

Alessia looked to him when Erik lowered the phone in his shaking hand. "I'm right there with you," she said, reaching over to give his forearm a squeeze in support. "The coven will help as well. You're not alone."

Before Erik could reply, his phone rang with Ben's tone. He felt his heart leap into his throat. "Ben—"

"Not exactly."

Erik froze at the unfamiliar voice and its heavy Russian accent.

"Who is this?"

"An old friend. We heard you were in town, and we thought we'd pay you a visit." The man's malicious chuckle sent a chill down Erik's back. "We've already met Ben. He's keeping us company, but you're the one we came to see."

"Ben has nothing to do with this." Erik caught Alessia's worried look. He tried to ease his grip on the phone so he didn't snap it in two. "Let him go."

"That's completely up to you, Erik. Did you really think that quitting your job meant we would forget?'

Erik closed his eyes and tried to breathe, knowing that the only way to save Ben would be to keep a clear head. "What do you want?"

"My boss would like a conversation with you. That's all."

Erik recognized the lie for what it was. His work with Interpol and other international law enforcement had cost the Mob and the oligarchs who backed them hundreds of millions of dollars, opened them to prosecution, and in some cases, led to extradition. He had been a fool to think he could just leave. Of course, his past would follow him, and Ben would pay the price.

"Ben has nothing to do with this."

"You surprise me, Erik. I propose a trade."

"I'm listening."

"Come alone. Give yourself up. No tricks. You walk in; he walks out. No one gets hurt."

Until later. Erik had no illusions about surviving his "meeting" with the caller's boss. He had cost them money, brought them under scrutiny, embarrassed them. There would be hell to pay.

Erik didn't care as long as Ben survived.

"Where and when?"

Alessia watched with concern. Erik couldn't guess her thoughts.

The caller named a time. "We'll call you to give you the rendezvous location. That way, you won't be tempted to invite outsiders."

"I'll be there. Just please, don't hurt Ben."

"Ben will be fine—as long as you do exactly as we say. Keep your phone on and wait for instructions." The call abruptly ended.

"They'll kill you." Alessia sounded surprisingly calm while Erik's heart hammered hard enough that he thought he might stroke out.

"I know."

"Ben wouldn't want you to walk into a trap."

"What choice do I have?" Erik slapped both hands on the steering wheel. "If I don't go, they'll kill Ben. They've been waiting for a chance to get to me. They aren't going to go away empty-handed."

"They're just men. Be smart about this," Alessia said. She sounded pissed, not scared. Not terrified like Erik felt.

"How? What do I do?" When threats came during his work with Interpol and the other agencies, Erik had backup. His superiors arranged for bodyguards. Erik found himself whisked away in SUVs with darkened windows surrounded by heavily armed men in body armor.

When he quit, protection stopped.

"You're not alone," Alessia repeated. "You have friends. We can help."

Erik nodded. "We need to bring Ben home safely."

"This isn't just about Ben."

Erik ducked his head. "I know. And if there's any way to protect myself and save Ben, I will. But if I have to choose—I brought this down on us. These are my chickens coming home to roost. I won't let Ben die because of it."

"You are soulmates. What do you think will become of him if they kill you?"

Erik stared at her. "What?"

Alessia met his gaze. "Did you think being soulmates was only about good sex? You have joined souls. You go; he goes sooner rather than later."

No. Erik's blood froze.

"Can you...magic his kidnappers away?"

Alessia shook her head. "No. More of them would come. But there are other ways to bring this to an end. Don't meet them alone."

Erik gave a curt nod, although his heart was in his throat. *They have Ben. They're going to kill Ben.*

"Let's go." He started the car and drove back to Trinkets. Lights glowed in the apartment upstairs, and he hoped Sean had stayed safe inside.

The two damaged cars had been towed away, leaving pebbled safety glass strewn across the now-empty parking space. Erik found a spot farther down the block and sat for a moment after he turned off the ignition. Alessia laid a hand on his arm.

"We saved Jaxon. We'll save Ben."

Erik swallowed. "I want to believe you. And I'm going to fight."

As soon as he and Alessia were safely inside the wards, Erik pulled out his phone. He dialed Tim's number, but the call went to voicemail.

"Tim, it's Erik. Bratva is here," he said, using the Russian name for organized crime. "They have my partner. If you intend to do anything, now would be a good time. You fucking owe me."

ELEVEN

BEN

"——As long as you do exactly as we say. Keep your phone on and wait for instructions." The older man ended the call and turned to Ben. His bodyguard remained a few steps away.

"Your 'partner' is smart. He agreed to our terms." Anatoly was clearly the boss. He gave orders, and the other men obeyed without delay.

"Go fuck yourself."

The big man, Vasili, backhanded Ben, snapping his head to one side with the force of the blow. "Show some respect," he growled.

Ben tasted blood from his split lip. His face throbbed from the punches he'd taken when he tried to make a break for it once the SUV stopped. They hadn't shot him. Knowing that they needed him for leverage with Erik, Ben had hoped they'd hold their fire. Vasili hadn't spared Ben a beating once he caught up and tackled him to the ground.

His teeth had cut into the inside of his cheek from one of the blows. Ben felt sure he'd cracked a couple of ribs after being landed on by a guy who was built like a linebacker. Vasili hadn't pulled his punches, and Ben ached all over. The bodyguard was a pro—he knew where to hit to cause pain without doing real damage...yet.

"Are you a cop, Ben Nolan? You don't seem like the 'real estate' type," Anatoly mused. "We have a little time before things become interesting to get to know each other."

Ben glared but stayed silent.

Anatoly didn't seem to expect an answer. "I'll go first. I am a businessman, running an import/export company. Sometimes, in the course of business, certain favors must be granted. Exceptions made. These things are difficult for outsiders to understand. So, they make judgments," he said with a shrug. "Jump to conclusions. Get in our way."

"Did Erik get in your way?" Ben already knew the answer. If he could keep Anatoly talking, it might be enough to distract him—at least for a little while.

Zip ties cut into Ben's wrists, holding them behind his back where breaking the plastic restraints was much harder. Other ties bound his ankles to the legs of his chair. Blood spattered his shirt and dirt streaked his jeans.

He had recognized the place as soon as the SUV stopped in front of a restaurant supply warehouse on the edge of town. It wasn't normally staffed except when deliveries or shipments were expected. By the time anyone discovered them, it would all be over.

The odds of both he and Erik getting out of this alive weren't good.

We have friends with...abilities. Erik's smart. He'll figure out a way to stop the Russians. It just might not be in time to save me.

Ben's job right now was to play for time. The longer Erik had to make a plan and gather allies, the more likely he was to win—and survive.

"Erik Mitchell cost me a very lucrative business deal," Anatoly replied. "I lost face to a prospective business partner I wished to impress. And then Mitchell dared to suspect me of having a hand in the disappearance of a trifling little statue, causing me no end of legal complications."

Ben's experience with mobsters gave him the ability to translate what Anatoly meant. *Erik was the expert witness who helped the authori-*

ties stop Anatoly's trade in stolen art. He identified a fraud Anatoly meant to sell to an oligarch for serious money. And he implicated Anatoly in that fucking figurine's theft, making the piece difficult to fence and reducing its value.

"He's out of the game. Why bother now?"

Anatoly swung his fist and cleared everything from a desk. "An example must be made. Others must learn such things will not be tolerated."

Typical mobster ego bullshit.

The desk was the sole piece of furniture aside from Ben's chair. Pallets full of boxes and bottles, many tightly wrapped in plastic sheeting, filled much of the space—supplies needed to keep the restaurants fully stocked to feed hungry tourists. Not far from where Ben sat, metal shelves stacked with bags of flour stood taller than Vasili.

Ben couldn't remember whether his captors had broken in or if someone knew the door code. His head hadn't quite cleared after being tackled, and everything was a little fuzzy. Anatoly and Vasili had been waiting for them in a sleek black Mercedes—that, he remembered.

"They'll find you. The cops already know about the food truck shakedowns."

Anatoly made a dismissive gesture. "I do not concern myself with that. It is nothing but pocket change. But in this case, it was the trucks that led us to your cousin, who brought us to Cape May. And that proved to be so very, very interesting."

One of the men who had helped kidnap Ben said something to Anatoly, who in turn went to have a quiet conversation in Russian on the other side of the open area. Vasili remained next to Ben, standing at parade rest.

Ben wished he could feel proud that they considered him potentially dangerous, but his stomach twisted with nerves at the backhanded compliment.

For a while, Anatoly seemed to forget about Ben. He made and received phone calls, gave orders to his associates, clicked his lighter, and chain-smoked Russian cigarettes. Their acrid smell battled with the scents of the baking and restaurant supplies.

A loud clanking sound filled the air and then a low droning followed. As soon as Ben felt the strong breeze, he realized it must be the HVAC—*maybe a dying one*, he thought. Even from a distance, he saw Anatoly's cigarette flare.

Ben didn't know how long they had been there. The storage building had no windows, and his head had taken a pounding, so he didn't completely trust his memories. Even so, Ben knew time was running out. Anatoly would call Erik with their location, offering a trade. Erik would accept the terms to save Ben.

Ben had no doubt Anatoly would kill them both.

He glanced up sharply as Anatoly made a call, figuring he was meant to overhear since the mobster had moved much closer.

"Meet us at the Saxon Restaurant Supply warehouse," Anatoly said. Ben wanted to shout for Erik to hear him, but Vasili closed his beefy hand around Ben's throat, squeezing just enough to restrict his air, warning him to be silent.

"Come alone. No police."

Erik must have spoken in agreement. Anatoly nodded. "Good. Smart man. Do as I say, and your partner will walk out of here alive."

"Don't do it, Erik!" Ben shouted, straining against his bonds and the hand that choked him. "He's lying—"

Vasili's hand closed tighter against his windpipe with calculated pressure. He knew just how hard to press, making Ben's world go gray around the edges, but not doing real damage.

"He still lives because I am generous," Anatoly cautioned Erik. "Do not try my patience." He ended the call. But instead of celebrating his win, the mobster lit another cigarette and paced, muttering in Russian.

Ben's eyes narrowed, assessing. Anatoly wasn't as secure in his power as he wanted to pretend. Would capturing Erik and delivering him to his bosses help Anatoly gain more power? Win forgiveness for the "inconveniences" Erik had caused in the past? Show up a rival?

He's vulnerable. This is his big play—nabbing Erik. He's betting the farm.

Win, and he redeems himself or beats his competition. Fail, and it's over. He's decided to go big or go home.

I want to send him home—in a body bag.

"Boss!" the driver of the SUV repeated his shout in Russian, followed up by a torrent of words in that language. Anatoly replied, speaking rapidly with an expression of supreme annoyance.

The only words Ben understood were "fuck" and "Newark."

For the first time, Vasili left his post beside Ben and strode toward where the others conferred. Ben had the feeling the shit had just hit the fan, and Anatoly's schemes might be coming undone.

Rossi was working for the Newark Mob, and the cops grabbed him. Did his bosses find out the Russians were here? Did they decide to send reinforcements?

What happens when the guys who want to kill you decide they want to kill each other more? Who is going to blink first?

They don't care if the cops show up. They just want a piece of each other.

Erik and I could get killed in the crossfire between two rival Mob factions. We're stuck between Godzilla and Mothra—and no matter who wins, we lose.

Anatoly's team prepared for war. Until now, Ben had only seen six men. Another five appeared at the boss's terse command and received their orders in rapid-fire Russian, heading to their posts with an impressive number of automatic weapons.

Ben thought about all the action movies he'd watched. He'd always focused on the hero's defiant swashbuckling and never stopped to think about the hostages who waited anxiously to find out whether they would live.

As his team took up battle stations, Anatoly paced, smoking like a chimney. Ben couldn't hold back a vindictive smile. Having the Newark rivals show up now threatened the Russians' victory. The Newark faction would focus on squashing an upstart rival's power. Erik meant nothing to them, although long memories might be interested in calling Ben to account for his undercover successes.

Newark was old guard, the Mob families that had been around since Capone made the headlines. By comparison, Anatoly and the

Brighton Beach crowd were the new kids, a threat to the long-established status quo. They were rough brawlers who paid no heed to the rules of *omertà*, gangster honor. Both groups were ruthless and deadly. The Russians didn't pretend to be anything but killers, while the old guard liked to pretend that they were gentleman rogues.

By Ben's estimation, Erik should arrive soon, and with Ben's life on the line, Erik wouldn't be late. *Just in time for World War Three.*

Vasili's phone went off. He answered, grunted a reply, and listened, then his head snapped up. "Boss. SWAT."

Ben grinned. Chief Hendricks might resent the excitement he and Erik brought to his quiet town, but when the chips were down, he came through. Sirens sounded in the distance.

I've got to do something...buy time. Ben looked around, gauging his options. They'd taken his gun and his phone. He couldn't use either with his hands tied, anyway. He tried again to free himself, feeling blood run hot and slick from where the plastic cut into his skin.

Ben eyed the shelves stacked with sacks of flour, only an arm's length away. If he threw himself to the side, he might be able to topple them. That would certainly split some bags open and fill the air with choking—and flammable—dust.

At least eight men with automatic weapons were positioned to fire at anyone who came in through the doors, while the others had gone to the roof. Reinforcements might save the day for the cops, but the first wave to arrive—surely including Erik—could pay with their lives.

He resolved to improve the odds for his would-be rescuers. *I've just got to wait for the right moment.*

At first, Ben thought he might be hallucinating. He heard the song from *Apocalypse Now*— Wagner's *Flight of the Valkyries*—growing louder by the second.

Anatoly answered a call, and Ben guessed it was from a scout on the roof. He couldn't catch most of the exchange, but one word stuck out—"UFO."

Ben's memory flashed on the tricked-out sound and effects system on Sean's food truck and his cousin's obvious pride in its capacity for blinding light shows and blaring music.

Sean, you wonderful moron!

A burst of automatic gunfire outside sobered Ben. *Sean!*

This was Ben's moment. The cavalry hadn't come over the hill yet. Sean's diversion drew the Russians' attention since their guard on the roof had apparently begun sharing a live video feed of what was happening outside with his windowless co-conspirators.

Even Vasili's attention was on his phone and not on Ben.

He realized luck might be with him as the HVAC kicked on, adding even more noise. Knowing he'd never get a better chance, Ben said a silent prayer for help, murmured a quiet apology to Erik for most likely hastening his own death, and made his move.

Ben hurled himself toward the metal shelving. He held his breath and closed his eyes as he and his chair hit the rickety shelves and sent them tumbling. The chair broke and bags of flour fell to the concrete floor, some popping open and others bursting like ripe fruit, sending white clouds into the air. The fans drew the flour up, spreading it.

Ben rolled, holding his breath, eyes shut tightly, his only goal to get out of the worst of the dust storm he had created.

He could hear the Russians coughing and shouting in confusion. Ben had gotten as far away as he could manage, but he couldn't hold his breath forever. He breathed as shallowly as possible, still keeping his eyes squeezed shut.

The first breath made him choke, coating the lining of his nose and throat. Ben wheezed, making it worse as he struggled to breathe deeper. He heard his captors gasping and gagging, coughing spasmodically and cursing between gasps.

Ben's gut roiled, and he barely made it onto his side before he heaved up everything in his stomach. The sound of men puking echoed in the cavernous warehouse, adding a new stench to the air. Then all the lights went out.

Magic, Ben thought, as he struggled to breathe and he gagged once more, dry heaving. *Erik brought reinforcements. Witches and food trucks to the rescue.*

He heard a voice on a bullhorn shouting orders to surrender, a crash as the doors broke open, and staccato gunfire inside the warehouse and in the distance. Then the flour in the air ignited.

I might be collateral damage, but I think we won. No matter what, Anatoly lost.

Ben wanted to enjoy the win, but consciousness slipped away, plunging him into darkness.

TWELVE

ERIK

"I'd feel a lot better about this if you had a Kevlar vest," Sean told Erik.

"Wouldn't do any good," Erik said. "These guys double-tap, back of the skull. Execution style. Brutal. Efficient."

Sean stared at him, eyes widening. "Holy shit. Ben wasn't pulling my leg about what you did before."

"No, he wasn't, unfortunately."

Sean's phone buzzed. "Monty's here. He can drop me off at the shed. Hanson is going to meet me there."

Erik clapped him on the shoulder. "You don't have to do this. You can sit it out."

"Hell, no. I told Ben I'd have his back when we were kids, and nothing's changed. Trust me—you'll see us coming," Sean assured him, then headed down the steps and hurried out to meet Monty.

"He's crazy," Alessia said, turning back toward Erik.

"That might be an advantage." Erik knew Sean needed to be part of the rescue attempt and wasn't about to begrudge him the chance, despite the danger. His plan wasn't that much more outlandish than what he and Alessia had in mind.

Sean's idea to include the pushy reporter from the courthouse was a stroke of genius. If the cops and the Feds failed them, streaming footage live on-air would force action—even if it came too late for Ben and Erik.

"Get any word from your old boss?" Alessia asked.

Erik shook his head, clenching his jaw at the feeling of disappointment and betrayal. "Didn't really expect I would."

"You alerted the police. Susan isn't going to let Chief Hendricks get away with anything short of full participation," Alessia reminded him. "And the coven is ready. I'll be their eyes and ears, and they will lend me their power."

Erik looked around the apartment. It felt much more like home when Ben was here to share it. *Without Ben...*he couldn't finish that thought.

This fight's been a long time coming. It ends now.

Erik drove alone. Alessia left separately after making him promise not to do anything stupid.

It's already too late for that.

The restaurant supply warehouse wasn't far. Still, the drive seemed to take forever. All Erik could think about was Ben. *Is he hurt? Is he still alive? Will he forgive me?*

When Erik had been in trouble, Ben charged to the rescue heedless of his own safety. Erik couldn't do any less.

Soulmates.

At first, Erik couldn't understand how strong his feelings were for a total stranger. He'd never been quick to form either friendships or romantic relationships, although taking things slow hadn't always guaranteed success. His cheating ex-boyfriend was proof of that.

Ben had been different from the first time they met. Erik couldn't put him out of his mind. The physical attraction was strong, but Erik knew from the start that this was more than just sex. Time deepened the connection. Ben had said the same. On some level, Erik had known their bond was unusual even before Alessia told him the truth. The way he and Ben were tangled up together so quickly, rooted so deep, was a once-in-a-lifetime thing. *Bone deep. Soul deep.*

Which made any other choice impossible.

Hang on, Ben. I'm coming.

Erik didn't see Alessia's car as he neared the warehouse, but he trusted that the witch had kept her word. He checked the time, noting he still had a few minutes until the deadline. Erik had no intention of testing the Russians' patience, but he held out hope that maybe help would arrive.

Foolishly optimistic to the very end.

Erik had done all the research that time permitted on the rendezvous location, looking at satellite photos and checking out the surrounding area. Anything to give himself the illusion of control. At least now he knew where all the doors were and the hiding places snipers were likely to be perched.

Armed with that information, Erik might live long enough to get inside.

If this went wrong, Erik hoped Ben would at least know that he came for him. Even if they never made it out of the warehouse, Erik needed Ben to understand that he kept his promise, that he wasn't going to leave Ben alone.

Soulmates belong together.

A black SUV and a sleek black Mercedes were parked in front. Obviously Bratva wasn't worried about blending in. A single security light struggled to illuminate the lot. The warehouse had no windows, but a glow leaked out around the doors.

Erik took a deep breath, squared his shoulders, and parked, leaving space between his car and the others. Just as he was about to get out, the thunderous chords of Wagner's *Flight of the Valkyries* boomed through the twilight.

Flashing lights nearly blinded him. They strobed and twinkled, changing color and pattern in a dizzying, random sequence, transforming Sean's boxy food truck into something fearsome and otherworldly as it hurtled toward the warehouse.

That's when Erik saw a woman holding up her cell phone, partially shielded by the open passenger-side door of the food truck, standing on the running board and holding on with one hand.

The reporter. My god, Sean—you're brilliant.

Shots fired.

Erik ducked, noting where the snipers were positioned on the roof. Hanson crouched but kept filming. Bullets hit the food truck, but it didn't slow, barreling toward the main doors. That gave Erik cover to run through the growing shadows since the snipers' attention was focused on the truck.

Sean's truck screeched to a halt seconds before plunging through the double doors, lights still flashing and Wagner deafeningly loud.

Step Two—it's the coven's turn.

With all attention on the food truck, Erik ran for the side door. He had to time his entry just right. Alessia and her witch sisters intended to cast a spell to disable everyone inside. That would include Ben, but she assured him the effects would be temporary, if unpleasant.

The sounds of coughing and retching were his clue. Erik dropped to his knees and picked the lock. *Damn, I'm out of practice.*

His head jerked up as sirens screamed, closer every second. In the sky, the beat of a helicopter's rotors made an odd counterpoint to the still-blaring Wagner.

Three squad cars, two fire engines, and a SWAT truck stormed into the parking lot. Between the flashing police lights and the food truck's strobes, it looked like an impromptu rave.

"Come out with your weapons down and your hands in the air," a deafeningly loud voice sounded from the helicopter circling overhead.

Erik tried to block out the noise and manipulate the lock tumblers. When it finally clicked, he stood partially shielded by the door as it opened, in case everyone's attention wasn't on the chaos at the front of the building.

A cloud of white dust nearly choked him, mingled with the sour smell of vomit. Flames raged at one end of the warehouse, and smoke filled the air. The warehouse was on fire.

Just as he was about to go in after Ben, a hand on his arm yanked him back. Erik rounded on the person, only to come face-to-face with Chief Hendricks, suited up in riot gear.

"The firefighters are going in, and we've also got a hazmat team,"

Hendricks said. "Don't know what happened, but I'm betting Ben pulled some damn-fool stunt."

"Hazmat? Ben's in there with no gear—"

"And if you charge in there, you'll be in his-and-his adjoining hospital rooms. Let us handle this," Hendricks ordered.

Erik's eyes watered, and his lungs protested. *Ben's inside. Can he breathe? Is he near the fire? Will he be okay?*

Erik went around to the front, just in time to see Sean shut down the music and lights as he and the reporter exited the food truck. She argued with one of the officers who tried to get her to turn off her camera, but Chief Hendricks waved the cop off with a resigned expression.

Just as Erik was about to join Sean, he saw a man in a dark suit striding across the lot.

"Tim? What the hell?"

"You are damn near impossible to protect, Mitchell. But I should have remembered that." Timothy Long was the same insufferable Fed Erik remembered, notable for being less dickish than many of his counterparts.

"I told you. My partner's in there." Erik chafed with the need to run inside and search for Ben. He saw the SWAT team and another group in white Hazmat suits heading into the warehouse along with firefighters, and for a second, he couldn't breathe, fearing the worst. Ambulances arrived, then more fire trucks. Screaming sirens made Erik's head feel like it might explode.

Please, let Ben be okay.

"Yeah. I get that," Tim replied. "You are a magnet for trouble, Mitchell. Only you could manage to have both Bratva and the Newark Mob converge on a fucking resort town on the same day."

"Newark?" Erik echoed.

"Yeah. You and your partner sure managed to piss off all the wrong people. We got a tip that some Newark goons were headed this way to settle a score with the Russians and intercepted them a couple of miles outside of town. Otherwise, this would look like the gunfight at the O.K. Corral."

"The Newark Mob? Weren't they after Ben?"

Tim chuckled. "Not this time—at least, I don't think he was their primary target, although they have a long memory. Nolan didn't endear himself when he helped cripple the Bianchi organization."

Of course, Tim researched Ben's history. Probably knows more than I do. He'd want to know all about the person his "asset" hooked up with. Erik wasn't sure whether to feel protected or violated.

"Nolan managed to turn over two valuable arrests even though he's not a cop anymore," Tim noted in a dry tone. "Impressive. Completely bonkers, but...helpful. One of them was a Bianchi Family associate, and the other had ties to Bratva—and is the likely suspect for sending the figurine to blow your cover here in Cape May."

Erik gave a half-smile. "I don't have a 'cover.' This isn't WITSEC."

"Makes me wonder if it needs to be."

Erik's head whipped toward his former boss, who wasn't joking. *I never thought I was that important—or in that much danger. But look what's happened here, because of me. They would all be safer without me. Would Ben go with me? Do I have a right to ask that of him?*

"He doesn't need WITSEC. He's got witches." Alessia came to stand beside Erik, and he could feel the energy still radiating from her. In his mind's eye, she glowed with power. He marveled that Tim seemed oblivious.

"Witches?" Tim's skeptical glance flicked between Erik and Alessia as if he was expecting a punchline.

"Welcome to Cape May," Erik replied with an enigmatic smile. "Nothing is as it appears."

A piercing whistle drew everyone's attention to Captain Hendricks, who was overseeing bodies on gurneys being loaded into ambulances. "Mitchell. Get over here."

"Gotta go," Erik said, relieved to end his conversation with Tim.

"Go get your guy." Tim shook his head in resignation. "We'll talk later."

Erik jogged across the parking lot to Hendricks, who stood beside Ben's gurney. The caked blood in Ben's hair and bruised face hinted at what he had endured.

"I'm here," Erik said, holding onto Ben's hand. They had him on a backboard, never a good sign. An oxygen mask fit over Ben's nose and mouth, and his eyes were covered.

"What's wrong?" Erik asked, staying next to the gurney as they headed for the ambulance.

"Someone knocked over shelves full of flour. Rough on the eyes and lungs—and surprisingly flammable," the EMT replied as they lifted Ben into the ambulance.

"You can ride with him to the hospital. We won't even ticket your car. This time," Hendricks said, a twitch of a smile.

"Thanks."

Erik climbed inside, kneeling beside Ben. "It's going to be okay," he said. "The worst is over. You're safe."

Ben squeezed his hand. "You?" The mask muffled his voice.

"Safe, too."

Ben relaxed, and Erik pulled back as far as possible to give the EMTs access while still holding Ben's hand. "I'm not going anywhere. Let them take care of you."

"Knew you'd come," Ben murmured. "Bought you time."

Ben must have knocked over the flour. Even though he knew he'd get hit with the effects. You brilliant, crazy, son of a bitch.

Erik watched the EMTs evaluate Ben, revealing bruised ribs and a possible concussion. It looked like he'd been worked over, and Erik's anger surged before he remembered that everyone who hurt Ben had been taken into custody.

When they reached the hospital, Erik reluctantly loosened his grip on Ben's hand. "I'll be waiting."

Ben squeezed his fingers. "Promise?"

"Promise."

Erik watched the EMTs wheel Ben into the Emergency Room, hanging back as triage teams swarmed. He looked up to find a desk nurse watching him with compassion.

"When can I talk to his doctor?" Erik asked.

"Are you family?"

Her reply felt like a bucket of cold water. "I'm his partner."

"Fiancé? Husband? Do you have health care power of attorney?"

Erik found himself tongue-tied. "No, but—"

"I'm sorry. But I can't provide information without the right paperwork. Federal law." She actually did seem remorseful.

"But I need to know—" Erik felt panic claw its way inside him. What if he couldn't get access to see Ben when he came back from treatment?

"I've got this." Sean bumped shoulders with Erik. "Ben's on the company policy. I talked to my mom on the way over. Ben and I gave each other Power of Attorney ages ago."

He cleared his throat. "Not like that can't change." Sean dug cards out of his wallet and slid them across the counter.

"Thanks for taking care of him."

"Always," Sean replied.

Erik gave him an assessing look. "Are you okay?"

Sean's cocky demeanor wasn't holding up well. "I mean, I'm here. That counts for something, right?"

"You were totally badass, back at the warehouse," Erik said sincerely.

"Yeah?"

"It was like *Close Encounters* meets *Apocalypse Now*, minus Devil's Tower and napalm," Erik assured him. "Although you're going to need some bodywork on the truck to get rid of those bullet holes."

"Are you fucking kidding?" Sean asked and nodded toward the TV screen behind the nurses' station. Footage from the bust was running, and from the captions, Erik saw the food truck name mentioned frequently. "That kind of street cred is gold. We'll be so badass we'll be lucky not to sell out every day before noon."

"Seriously?" Protectiveness bloomed in Erik's chest. Had Sean used Ben's near-death experience for promotion?

"Chill, dude. I made a deal with the reporter, just like I said I would. She streamed the situation live and got it into an on-air rotation—to force the powers that be to take it seriously, if they weren't already—and I got her a front-row seat to the biggest bust in Cape May history," Sean said. "If she's name-dropping, that's all on her."

Erik relaxed, breathing a sigh of relief. "You certainly did make an impression."

Sean grinned. "I always do." He paused. "By the way, if you're serious about wanting some ink, my friend Mateo will give you the family discount. Seeing how you're my cousin's partner. Welcome to the family."

While they waited for news, Sean convinced Erik to ask for eyewash and cold water to soothe his burning eyes and raw throat, a result of his brief exposure at the warehouse. Erik got a look at himself in the mirror. He couldn't blame the red eyes completely on the dust in the air at the restaurant supply since he had fought tearing up the entire time he was in the ambulance with Ben.

I can't break down now. I need to be strong for Ben. Later, once he's okay...then I can fall apart.

When he came back to the waiting area, Sean held out a hot cup of coffee. "Figured you'd need it," he said, and Erik managed a smile in gratitude.

"I do. But it's gonna burn like a mofo going down," Erik replied, surprised at the roughness of his voice.

"No one's been by with an update," Sean told him. "I asked before I went to get coffee."

"Thanks." Erik wasn't sure how long his voice would hold out, and he wanted to be able to ask questions or talk to Ben.

Sean guzzled his coffee and set the empty cup by his feet, clasping his hands between his knees. He kept his gaze on his hands as he spoke. "I've known Ben all my life. I've never seen him like this with anyone else. He cares about you a lot. And until now, life's kicked him in the teeth. So just...don't hurt him." His tone was a plea and a threat. "I'd have to come bust your ass."

Erik believed him. "I love him. I'm going to do my best to take good care of him." He sighed. "Great job I've done so far."

"We both brought the Russians to town, so him getting nabbed is as much on me as on you," Sean said. "Now we just have to get him through this."

"I'm not going anywhere." Erik had already considered—and

discarded—Tim's WITSEC comment, still not sure whether Tim had been serious. Nowhere would ever be completely safe, but in Cape May, they had friends—and allies.

Once he had learned about Trinket's covert role in helping to stop supernatural threats, Erik had the feeling that he'd been meant to take over the shop. Maybe he'd even been selected and nudged, given the conversation he'd had with Sorren, the vampire who was now an unusual business partner. *I think I'm where I'm meant to be. Running Trinkets—with Ben.*

Once Erik's mind cleared from the fog of the fight, he realized that he needed to give Sorren an update—especially since the news channels seemed to be running the food truck/UFO segment on repeat. He wandered down the hallway until he was out of earshot from Sean and placed the call. To his surprise, Sorren picked up.

"Erik. Tell me what's going on." The worry in the vampire's voice surprised Erik.

"I'm at the hospital, waiting to see Ben. He caused a distraction that saved a lot of lives, but he got hurt in the process. Teag and your other friends were a huge help. We couldn't have come up with the banishing spell for the theater *strega* without them."

"Teag and Rowan have been keeping me apprised," Sorren replied, and Erik tried not to think about how strange it was to be talking on a cell phone to a nearly six-hundred-year-old vampire. "I'm glad you're okay."

"I won't really be all right until I know how Ben is," Erik confessed. "But thanks." He ended the call and headed back to where Sean sat, just as a woman in scrubs and a white coat walked toward them.

"Mr. Nolan?"

Sean and Erik both rose. "That's me," Sean said.

"I'm Doctor Flinn," the woman said. From the exhaustion in her face, Erik wondered if she had pulled a double shift.

"How's my cousin?"

The doctor's gaze flickered to Erik, questioning.

"He's Ben's partner," Sean said. "It's okay."

Dr. Flinn nodded. "He's stable. The flour and smoke in the air caused serious irritation to exposed mucous membranes, including the lungs. Apparently, he managed to be out of the worst of it—and a distance from the fire—so the damage isn't as bad as it could be." She shook her head. "Some of the others who came in weren't as lucky."

"Damage?" Erik echoed. "Will it heal?"

Ben protected himself because he's the one who knocked over the flour. That was his "Hail Mary pass" to buy time. Dammit!

"His eyes and the lining of his mouth, nose, sinuses, and throat are going to be sore for a while. I've prescribed medicine to speed the healing and prevent infection. I don't think there'll be congestion in his lungs, but we'll have to watch. Breathing treatments will help. And no activity that puts stress on his lungs until he's healed," she added.

"That's good advice for his cracked ribs too," Dr. Flinn continued. "The rest of the injuries aren't serious, although they're going to hurt, and he'll probably have some spectacular bruises in a day or so. Ice will help."

Erik nodded, paying full attention. "Okay. I'll make sure all that happens. Is he awake? Can we see him?"

Dr. Flinn nodded. "He's on painkillers to relieve the discomfort and oxygen for a little while longer to make it easier for him to breathe. He should be waking up soon. We rinsed his eyes thoroughly, but just to be on the safe side, there are drops to numb them and more drops to prevent infection. He'll need to wear dark glasses at all times and avoid eye strain until the irritation heals. I'd like to keep him at least overnight for observation. If an infection does set in anywhere, we want to catch it right away."

"Understood. Can I stay with him?"

She shrugged. "That's not up to me. You'll have to ask the armed cop standing guard outside his door."

Dr. Flinn led them to Ben's room, where an officer was on watch. Erik and Sean showed ID, and apparently Chief Hendricks had already set up an approved list of visitors because the cop waved them in.

Erik caught his breath when he saw Ben lying in bed, paler than usual, where he wasn't bruised and bloodied. He had a black eye and a few cuts—and likely more injuries Erik couldn't see. Monitors checked Ben's heart and breathing, and an oxygen mask covered his nose and mouth. Ben's wrists were bandaged where the zip ties had cut into his flesh. Sean hung back as Erik approached the bed.

"God, Ben. I'm so sorry." Ben didn't stir.

Erik gingerly took Ben's hand. "Sean and I are here. And we'll stay with you, even if they try to throw us out."

"After seeing the way you took on the Mob tonight, I'm not going to try to make you leave. You'd probably crawl back in the window." Chief Hendricks stood in the doorway, looking worse for the wear after a long night.

"Sounds likely," Sean agreed.

"Did you get the guys who took Ben?" Erik hoped to hell the Russians were in custody so he and Sean could stop looking over their shoulders—at least for now.

"They're here in the hospital under heavy guard in another wing," Hendricks said. "I didn't expect Nolan to spring for low-tech chemical warfare. We're guessing that the flour blinded and choked them—then something set off an explosion. We may never know what. The Bratva boys aren't going anywhere for a while—at least not until they stop coughing up blood and get skin grafts for the burns."

Erik shivered, realizing that Ben's injuries could have been far worse.

"And the Newark crowd?" Erik asked.

Hendricks shrugged. "Your Fed buddy took them. Said he'd come back for another load when the Russians can travel. I imagine we'll both be doing paperwork until then."

"I was afraid we were going to be on our own."

Hendricks looked like he intended to make a smart remark, then took in Erik's sober expression and seemed to reconsider. "And you were still going in?"

Erik and Sean nodded. "Of course," Erik said.

Hendricks pinched the bridge of his nose. "This used to be a quiet little town."

"Nah," Sean replied. "This kind of thing has always happened—

people just pretended they didn't notice. Thanks for doing something about it."

Hendricks sighed. "Even with the Hazmat suits, two of my team are benched with injuries. We were lucky to get an assist from the chopper, or the snipers could have done some real damage. You guys don't do anything by halves, do you?"

"We'll do our best to stay out of trouble," Erik promised.

"Yeah. I'll believe that when I am blissfully bored. We're not only crawling with Feds right now, but every reporter in the state is trying to get an interview." Hendricks turned his glare on Sean, who had the good grace to flinch, then looked up defiantly.

"We didn't know that the police or the Feds would have our backs," Sean said. "Emma Hanson made sure everyone knew what was going on, so that even if we failed, what happened couldn't be hidden."

Hendricks held Sean's gaze, but the clench of his jaw signaled the effort to rein in his temper. "I can't change how things were run in the past. But some of us have every intention of doing things differently in the here and now."

He and Sean stayed locked in a staring match until Erik thought one of them would throw a punch.

"I hope you can make that work," Sean said. "A lot of people are counting on it. And...thanks for pulling our asses out of the fire."

"That's what we're here for when we do our jobs right," Hendricks replied. Something shifted, and the tension between them eased. Sean nodded in agreement, and Hendricks's shoulders relaxed, no longer ready for a fight.

Hendricks turned to Erik. "An officer will be in the hallway 24/7 until Ben leaves the hospital. I'll probably put a car in front of your house for a week, just to be sure the threat's gone—so pick one place for both of you. Saves me having to tie up two officers on babysitting duty."

"We'll be at my place," Erik said. "That way, Susan can keep an eye on us too."

Hendricks shook his head in fond frustration. "Don't even... She saw the news coverage. I had to assure her you both were alive and in reasonably good shape to keep her from marching in here with chicken soup. Expect your freezer to be full of casseroles when you get home."

The chief headed back to the station, leaving Sean and Erik alone with Ben. Erik worried that Ben hadn't stirred throughout the whole conversation with Hendricks.

"Ben? Can you hear me?" Erik gave Ben's hand a gentle squeeze. Sean pulled two plastic guest chairs closer to the bed.

"How about I run down to the cafeteria and see if I can get us some sandwiches?" Sean said. "Don't know about you, but I'm starving."

Erik nodded, knowing that Sean was giving him time alone with Ben. "Sure. Thank you. I'll get the next round."

After Sean left, Erik leaned in to kiss Ben on his unbruised cheek. "You scared the shit out of me tonight," he confided in a voice just above a whisper. "Even with the witches, I thought we were going to be way outnumbered. Hendricks came through—and so did my old boss. Sean was badass. I'm just happy we got you back."

Ben stirred, and gave Erik's hand a squeeze.

"You're going to be okay, if you weren't awake for that part of the conversation. Gonna feel like crap for a while, but the doc thinks there's no permanent damage. And...don't freak out...you've got drops in your eyes and sunglasses on." He snickered. "You look like a rock star who got in a fight with the paparazzi."

Erik took a sip of his now-cold coffee. "Arjun called—Jaxon is okay. Alessia and I banished the *strega's* ghost. No more curse." *God, was that only this afternoon?* Erik felt like days had passed.

"Erik?" Ben's voice sounded like he had gargled glass.

"I'm right here."

"Did you get hurt?" Erik had to lean closer to pick up the words spoken in a rough whisper.

"No. I'm fine. Don't worry about me. Just rest, and get better."

"Can we go home?"

Erik lifted Ben's hand to his lips and kissed his knuckles. "Not tonight. Docs need to keep an eye on you for a while."

"Stay?"

"Of course. Sean and I will sit with you, and there's a cop in the hallway. You're safe. We're together. It'll be okay."

Home. Ben's word choice made Erik blink as the truth hit him. *Home is where we're together.* There was no reason to put off asking Ben to move in, and Erik couldn't remember why he had delayed.

"Once you feel better, I want to talk about sharing the apartment," Erik said. He'd have to repeat the conversation when Ben was more lucid, but Erik figured he might as well put the idea out for discussion.

"I'd like that," Ben murmured.

The painkillers were dragging Ben back under, and his voice slurred. Erik gently pushed Ben's hair back from his forehead and kissed him. "Together," Erik promised.

THIRTEEN

BEN

"Ever since that reporter rode Sean's food truck into battle, he's been social media famous," Ben said, flipping through pictures on his phone. "My cousin, the celebrity."

"Have you seen all the pictures people took standing next to the bullet holes?" Erik called from the kitchen. "He's living large."

"It's been good for business," Ben said. "The shine might wear off eventually, but he's definitely this season's star. I'm glad. He worked hard for it. And he helped you save my ass," he added, grinning.

"At least the protection money goons backed off," Erik replied. "I don't know whether they think he helped save their guys from the Newark Mob or that he has an in with the Feds, but he's bulletproof—at least for now."

In the week since the shootout at the warehouse, Erik, Ben, and Sean had moved all of Ben's things from the rental unit into Erik's apartment. Ben's Spider-Man statue and Marvel posters found their place between Erik's art prints and figures of the Egyptian gods. The culture clash shouldn't have worked, but it was perfect—just like the chemistry between Ben and Erik.

Erik made sure Ben got his medicine and brought him to the

hospital for breathing treatments. Ben did his best to be a good patient, but compliance had never been his strong suit.

"The sunglasses look badass," Erik teased.

"Only douchebags wear sunglasses inside."

"I think you look hot."

"Oh yeah?" Ben replied. His ribs and lungs were healing, but anything strenuous was still prohibited. That meant he and Erik had been limited to making out like teenagers, hand jobs and frot, more foreplay than enthusiastic love making. It took the edge off, and Ben had learned to appreciate the pleasure of going slow, but he missed more rambunctious sex.

When you're better, we can go fast again. Erik's words echoed in his mind. Ben smiled, thankful for a partner willing to accommodate.

How did I get so lucky? Erik is everything I wanted, even when I didn't know what I needed.

"Are you sure you're up to this? It's waited almost seventy years. It can wait another week," Erik said, pulling Ben from his thoughts.

"Bowers is old. He could die, and then we never get the answers," Ben replied.

"We could make the trip and still not get answers."

"It's worth trying." Ben knew Erik meant to protect him, but he'd been wanting to confront Robert Bowers about the car bombing since Jon and Monty had put the pieces together. "He's probably the one who sent the twisted metal to the Arts Council. Don't you want to know?"

Erik stilled. "What difference will it make?"

"It matters to Monty—and Jon. He's the last piece of Jon's story. Even if no one else knows—we will."

After a moment, Erik nodded. "Okay. Anna can cover the store." Anna had started working part time when she wasn't at the Center for the Arts. Susan had filled their freezer with casseroles like her son had predicted while Ben was in the hospital, and she and Anna often handled Trinkets so Erik could spend time helping Ben with his doctor appointments. "Let's go."

Robert Bowers lived a half-hour outside Cape May, in the same house he owned since his movie-making days. When Erik pulled up in front of the small bungalow, he narrated what he saw since Ben's vision still wasn't back to normal.

"Small house—snug but not in the best shape. Not a surprise—the guy is older than God," Erik said. "Monty just parked behind us."

Monty hesitated after he got out of his truck. Susan drove him, so Monty could channel Jon and contain the ghost inside his body. Ben hadn't realized that Monty could do that. Monty confessed that he couldn't let Jon ride him for very long, but a few hours wouldn't be too much. Jon couldn't go far beyond the lighthouse on his own, but something about Monty allowing Jon to ride shotgun in his mind seemed to extend the ghost's range.

"Something wrong?" Erik asked. Ben appreciated that Erik voiced routine comments, sparing his still-healing throat.

"Jon's nervous," Monty replied. "He knew Bowers, remember? It's just a bit much."

"You're not alone," Erik said. "And Bowers can't hurt you now."

Erik led the way to the bungalow's door. He knocked, with Ben and Monty standing on the sidewalk, far away enough to not be intimidating.

"Who are you?" The old man who opened the door didn't look like Ben's idea of a car bomber. Then again, Ben reminded himself, Bowers had gotten one of his old army buddies to do the dirty work.

"Hello, Robert." The voice came from Monty, but it wasn't his normal tone.

Bowers squinted, staring hard at Monty. "Do I know you?"

"You did. I'm Jon Richards."

Bowers recoiled. "What game are you playing? Richards has been dead for a long time. Get out of here—or I'll call the cops."

"We know you arranged for the car bomb that killed Vincente Cafaro," Erik said quietly, and Bowers's head snapped to look at him, and then his gaze raked over Ben and Monty. "We want to talk."

"Come inside."

They sat awkwardly on Bowers's sagging couch. The house

smelled of cheap cigarettes and liniment. Bowers himself was skin and bones, pale as a corpse. "What do you want?"

"The truth," Erik said. "About what happened to Cafaro."

Bowers barked a harsh laugh. "Everything that happened to Cafaro was what he deserved."

"You got one of your army buddies to set the charges, didn't you?" Jon spoke through Monty. "They always did what you said."

"Prove it." Bowers might have one foot in the grave, but he remained defiant.

Erik shrugged. "This isn't about turning you in. Jon's ghost's been waiting a long time to solve the puzzle. You can give him the last piece."

Bowers regarded Monty with cold blue eyes. "Jon Richards died a long time ago," he repeated, but this time, he sounded uncertain.

"Never said he didn't," Monty replied. "Doesn't mean he's gone."

Bowers reached for a pack of cigarettes and lit up without a by-your-leave. "Cafaro was a monster. He murdered Voorhis. Corella. Duncan. Richards. He pretty much killed the whole fucking local movie industry. I had no star, no stunt director, no producer. The theater was in chaos. Our backers fled. I had nothing. *Nothing!*"

Despite his age, Bowers's rage had not abated. His eyes burned with hatred, and spittle flew from his lips. "No one wanted to film here in Cape May anymore. And nobody would hire me. TV was just getting started. There wasn't enough work for them to need me. Video was a long way off. Hell, even the pornos wouldn't hire me to direct. I ended up doing odd jobs, mowing lawns, bagging groceries. Anything to put food on the table. All because of Cafaro."

"Did you send the piece of twisted metal to the Arts Council?" Erik asked.

The old man's thin features twisted into a snarl. "I wanted them to back off. To remember that Cafaro was a *monster*. He and Voorhis were scum. They don't deserve an exhibit about the Regent Theater. Cafaro destroyed everything. Not just for me, but for the whole town. I wanted to send a message."

"Message received," Erik said.

"That's it?" Bowers said. "That's what you came for? You're not going to try to haul me off to the cops, turn me in to the Feds? Because it won't do you any good. I've got terminal colon cancer. Dead man walking. So, knock yourselves out. Execute me—it would be a kindness."

"You lived decades longer than we did," Jon said through Monty. "Years and years that Jason and I didn't have together. And you wasted all of it."

Monty stood and gave a nod to Ben and Erik. "We're through."

Bowers took a long drag on his cigarette and let them see themselves out.

Ben and Erik followed Monty to their cars. Susan gave Erik an inquiring look through the windshield of Monty's car, and Erik nodded to let her know they'd gotten what they came for. "I'm sorry," Erik said, sure he spoke for Ben as well.

Monty shrugged. "There was no way it could have gone better." This time, his voice was his own. "But now we know for sure."

Erik clapped a hand on Monty's shoulder. "Will Jon be okay?"

Monty nodded. "Yeah. He's with me. We'll be fine."

Erik and Ben watched them drive away and got into Erik's car. "It's funny how Jon could lose his lover and be murdered, then spend decades wandering around as a ghost—and be able to fall in love and start over. While Bowers—" Erik's voice trailed off.

"Bowers has been dead inside for a long time," Ben replied. "Jon came out ahead if you ask me. What about Cafaro?"

"I'll get Alessia to stop by the Center for the Arts with me tomorrow and see if we can give Cafaro's ghost closure too," Erik said. "He's tied to that old clock you found. If he needs a nudge to go to the afterlife and not come after Bowers, Alessia can handle that."

They were quiet on the drive back. Erik reached over to take Ben's hand, and Ben tangled their fingers together. *We're together and alive. It's a gift. And I intend to make the most of it.*

Erik took over for Anna at the store when they got back, and Ben opted to hang out in the break room to keep him company. He thought about his first visit to Trinkets and how strange the shop and its mix of curios and antiques had seemed to him.

Now the store felt like home because Erik was here. Susan had adopted both of them, and Ben had to admit he didn't mind a little mothering. *Better late than never.*

He loved watching Erik in his element, whether discussing the history of an object with a customer or writing up posts for the blog that was part of his online Treasure Trail store. Erik brought a quiet passion to everything he did, and Ben felt grateful to know how that enthusiasm played out in every aspect of their lives.

"Time to close up shop," Erik said, wandering into the break room. He glanced around, then looked back at Ben. "You didn't have to wash the coffee pot. I would have done that."

Ben shrugged and realized his ribs protested less than usual, a sign that he was healing. "You were busy with a customer, and I figured it would help us blow this popsicle stand a little faster."

"Thanks." Erik grabbed his laptop from the office and made a final check to ensure everything was turned off. "I'm starving. I put a frozen lasagna in the oven an hour ago. It should be ready right about now."

Ben walked out the door, and Erik paused to lock up behind him. He could smell tomato sauce and basil in the hallway. His stomach rumbled.

"Try not to starve to death before we get to the top of the steps," Erik said with a laugh. "If you want garlic bread and a salad, that'll take a few minutes longer."

"I might not make it," Ben joked. "I'm still recovering. Need to eat to keep up my strength."

Erik pulled him into his arms. "How about we go eat a nice, quiet dinner, and then I'll run a hot bath. There's room for both of us to soak together, even if you're not up to anything more...gymnastic... just yet."

"That sounds persuasive," Ben teased, loving the way Erik's eyes lit up when he flirted.

"Uh-huh," Erik replied, stealing a kiss. "Then afterward, once you're warm and relaxed, I'll give you a massage to work on those sore muscles…complete with a *very* happy ending."

"*Very* happy?" Ben could do his share of flirting too.

"Extremely happy." Erik kissed Ben on the temple while one hand slipped lower to cup his groin. "Satisfaction guaranteed."

"I like that," Ben murmured. He had his thigh between Erik's legs, and from the way Erik had chubbed up, he wondered if his partner had a thing for Ben's new gravelly voice. He'd willingly recreate the growl after he recovered if it got Erik hot and hard.

"I'm glad you moved in," Erik said, pulling Ben close for one more kiss before stepping back so they could head upstairs. "It feels like home when you're here."

Ben felt his heart swell. *Home.* "I'm home when I'm with you," he said, silently promising himself that he would do everything in his power to make that arrangement permanent. "Now—how about that lasagna?"

AFTERWORD

I hope you enjoyed learning more about Erik and Ben. If you haven't read *Trick or Treat at Caynham Castle*, my contribution is *Secrets and Ciphers*, a holiday novella that takes place after the events in this book starring Erik and Ben on a trip to England.

Psychic medium Simon Kincaide stars in his own series, Badlands, set in Myrtle Beach, where he teams up with a skeptical homicide cop to solve supernatural murders. Brent Lawson and his partner Travis Dominick have their own series as well, The Night Vigil, starting with *Sons of Darkness* (written under my Gail Z. Martin name). Teag, Sorren, Donnelly, and Rowan are part of my Deadly Curiosities series (also written as Gail Z. Martin).

All of my modern-day series as Morgan Brice and Gail Z. Martin overlap, and the characters know each other, help each other, and show up in each other's books.

Cape May holds a special place in my heart. I'm looking forward to the continuing adventures of Ben and Erik!

Thank you for reading. Because you read, I write.

ACKNOWLEDGMENTS

Thank you so much to my editor, Jean Rabe, to my husband and writing partner Larry N. Martin for all his behind-the-scenes hard work, and to my wonderful cover artist Lou Harper, and to Mindy, Barb, Stacy, Andrea, and Kirk for their help. Thanks also to the Shadow Alliance and the Worlds of Morgan Brice street teams for their support and encouragement, and to my fantastic beta readers: Andrea, Chris, George, Jeanne, Laurie, Pavel, and Sandra, plus my promotional crew and the ever-growing legion of ARC readers who help spread the word, including: Anne, Ashby, Ashley, Ben, Dawn, Debbie, Grace, Harrison, Jamie, Janet, Janneke, Jay, Jennifer, Karen, Karolina, Kathy, Ken, Kimberly, Kristen, Laurie, Mary, Melissa, Sara, Tammi, Terry, and Tracey—couldn't do it without you! Special thanks to Pavel for asking questions about the Cafaro incident that led to the addition of a whole plot thread! And of course, thanks and love to my "convention gang" of fellow authors for making road trips fun.

ABOUT THE AUTHOR

Morgan Brice is the romance pen name of bestselling author Gail Z. Martin. Morgan writes urban fantasy male/male paranormal romance, with plenty of action, adventure, and supernatural thrills to go with the happily ever after.

Gail writes epic fantasy and urban fantasy, and together with co-author hubby Larry N. Martin, steampunk and comedic horror, all of which have less romance and more explosions.

On the rare occasions Morgan isn't writing, she's either reading, cooking, or spoiling two very pampered dogs.

Watch for additional new series from Morgan Brice and more books in the Witchbane, Badlands, Treasure Trail, Kings of the Mountain, and Fox Hollow universes coming soon!

Where to find me, and how to stay in touch

Join my Worlds of Morgan Brice Facebook Group and get in on all the behind-the-scenes fun! My free reader group is the first to see cover reveals, learn tidbits about works-in-progress, have fun with exclusive contests and giveaways, find out about in-person get-togethers, and more! It's also where I find my beta readers, ARC readers, and launch team! Come join the party! https://www.Facebook.com/groups/WorldsOfMorganBrice

Find me on the web at https://morganbrice.com. Sign up for my newsletter and never miss a new release! http://eepurl.com/dy_8oL. You can also find me on Twitter: @MorganBriceBook, on Pinterest (for Morgan and Gail): pinterest.com/Gzmartin, on Instagram as

MorganBriceAuthor, and on Bookbub https://www.bookbub.com/authors/morgan-brice

Enjoy two free short stories set in Fox Hollow: Nutty for You—https://claims.prolificworks.com/free/r54nldjv and Romp—https://claims.prolificworks.com/free/I4lCYKli

Check out the ongoing, online convention ConTinual www.facebook.com/groups/ConTinual

Support Indie Authors

When you support independent authors, you help influence what kind of books you'll see more of and what types of stories will be available, because the authors themselves decide which books to write, not a big publishing conglomerate. Independent authors are local creators, supporting their families with the books they produce. Thank you for supporting independent authors and small press fiction!

ALSO BY MORGAN BRICE

Badlands Series

Badlands

Restless Nights, a Badlands Short Story

Lucky Town, a Badlands Novella

The Rising

Cover Me, a Badlands Short Story

Loose Ends

Leap of Faith, A Badlands/Witchbane Novella

Night, a Badlands Short Story

No Surrender

Fox Hollow Zodiac Series

Huntsman

Again

Fox Hollow Universe

Romp

Nutty for You

Imaginary Lover

Haven

Gruff

Kings of the Mountain Series

Kings of the Mountain

Treasure Trail Series

Treasure Trail

Blink